Ride the High Sierra

Raymond D. Mason

Ride the High Sierra
(Sackett Series #11)

Copyright © 2015 by Raymond D. Mason
Published by Raymond D. Mason
Edited by Lance Knight

All rights reserved. No part of this book may be used or reproduced by any means, graphic, electronic, or mechanical; including photocopying, recording, taping or by any information storage retrieval system without the written permission of the publisher/author except in the case of brief quotations embodied in critical articles and reviews.

Raymond D. Mason books may be ordered through authorized booksellers associated with Mason Books or by contacting:

You may order books through:
www.Amazon.com
www.BandN.com
www.Borders.com
www.CreateSpace.com
www.Target.com

or personalized autographed copies from:
E-mail: RMason3092@aol.com

(541) 679-0396

For Editing Services:
Muser4you@gmail.com

This is a work of fiction. All characters, names, incidents, organizations, and dialogue in this novel are either the products of the author's imagination or are used fictitiously.

Printed in the United States of America

Preface

Brent and Brian Sackett were identical twins who had fought in the Civil War on opposite sides. When the War was over Brian returned to the family cattle ranch in Texas, but Brent, still bitter over the family siding with the North, refused to come home. Instead he became a lawman turned outlaw.

While pursuing two men who had shot their oldest brother, AJ Sackett, Brian accidentally ran across Brent in San Antonio, Texas. It was there that he found out his brother was on the run from the law.

Although their meeting was brief Brian could tell that Brent still held a lot of animosity and anger towards his family. After the two had parted company Brent happened across a family that had been making a move to Sundown, Texas when they were attacked by a ruthless cattle owner's men. The men in the family had all been killed, but the wife of one of the men was still alive.

Brent took her to the nearest doctor he could find and promised her that he would take her on to Sundown, Texas to the farm her husband had purchased.

The woman's husband had not been a good husband. She saw goodness in Brent she had never seen in her husband. Before they arrived in Sundown the two had fallen in love. The woman, Julia, was the best thing that had ever happened to Brent and he began to change his evil ways.

Through a series of events, Brent, Brian and AJ had reconnected and patched things up, for the most part anyway. Brent told them he was going out to California where he could get a fresh start and hopefully the law wouldn't find him there. The brothers said goodbye to one another and went their separate ways. Brian and AJ returned to the family ranch while Brent and Julia headed west.

Along the way they picked up a man who'd lost his wife and was caring for his newborn baby. Not long after that they found two children whose adopted parents had been murdered by an outlaw gang. When they ran across the gang they rescued a woman held captive by the outlaws. During the melee, however, Julia was killed by a bullet from one of the outlaws.

Brent was heart broken over the loss of the only woman he'd truly loved. At one point, Brent left the others to fend for themselves and struck out on his own. Realizing his leaving them would not be what Julia would have him do, he returned to see they all made it out to California safely.

They had just crossed into California, however, when Brent was recognized by two Texas Rangers. They were on the trail of another man when they accidentally met up with Brent. When one of the rangers recognized him, he was arrested and thrown into a makeshift jail at a place called Knox's Corner.

Meanwhile, Brent's identical twin brother, Brian had met a woman while they were being held prisoner by a gang of Comancheros and he too had fallen in love. When their romance ended rather abruptly Brian took a job as a railroad detective and left the family cattle ranch.

It was Brian's hope to forget the woman he'd fallen deeply in love with by getting as far away from her as he could. The young lady, however, still loved Brian, but the hurt he'd felt wouldn't allow him to see it.

When Brian left the family ranch he had no idea if or when he would return. His father, John Sackett and the oldest Sackett sibling, AJ, would have to run the ranch without Brian's help. This would lead to trouble down the road because of several enemies the Sackett's had made over the years.

One of those enemies was a man Brian had met during the War Between the States by the name of Cable Dutton. The two had a run in over Dutton's mistreatment of prisoners they were escorting to their headquarters for questioning.

Dutton had whipped one of the men unmercifully with a small tree limb. When Brian saw him he had stepped in to stop him and the two men got into a fight. During the fight Dutton was hit in the right eye and lost sight in it.

Dutton, a huge man, had held this injury against Brian ever since and had vowed vengeance. After the War Dutton had joined a gang of outlaws that robbed a number of banks, stagecoaches, and were then setting their sights on trains. The latter would once again bring the two men face to face.

Our story opens with Brent Sackett preparing to leave a farmhouse he had happened upon where he found the entire family down with the fever. Brent managed to escape from the makeshift jail where the Texas Rangers had left him locked up. He knew he had to get as far away from the area as he could.

Brent was bound for northern California where he could meet up once again with those he had escorted out to the Golden State. His destination was Sacramento, California. It was a long journey from where he was at that time.

Chapter 1

Braden Farm
October 31, 1879

Brent saddled the palomino stallion he had taken when he escaped from jail. As he prepared to leave the Braden farm Luke Braden, the youngest son of Steve and Mary Braden, hung on the corral fence and watched him. Luke was wearing a sad look on his little freckled face as Brent pulled the cinch tight on the palomino.

"I don't know why you have to go, Mr. Jones. Ma and Pa sure do like you...and Ben and me, well, you know we want you to stay," Luke said.

"Well, I'll tell you, Luke. I'd like nothin' better than to just stay right here and go fishing with you and Ben everyday, but I've got to be movin' on," Brent said with a grin and then added. "Did you forget I said you could call me Jim?

"When I'm a wantin' someone to do somethin' I always call them 'mister' or 'sir'. My mama said you can get folks to do just about anything if you'll ask them real nice like," Luke said. "That's why I'm askin' you real nice."

Brent chuckled at Luke's honesty and replied, "I wish I could stay, but I've got people waitin' for me up north. I'll tell you what, though. The next time I get down this way I'll be sure and come see you; is that a deal?"

"D'you promise?"

"I promise! Now run and get me my 'war bags' would you? I left them on the front porch," Brent said with a warm smile.

Luke jumped down off the fence and ran towards the house. Just as Luke picked up the saddlebags the door opened and Mary Braden stepped out onto the porch. She looked towards the corral and then down at Luke.

"I'll take that out to Mr. Jones, Luke," she said softly.

"But he told me to get it, Ma," Luke said with a slight frown.

"You go in and get that sack of homemade biscuits I made for him to take on his journey. They're on the table," Mary said.

While Luke went to fetch the biscuits Mary carried the saddlebags to the corral where Brent was just tying his bedroll on behind the saddle. As she approached Brent looked in her direction and smiled.

"It's good to see all of you up and walking around and looking like pictures of health," Brent, alias Jim Jones said.

"I don't know what we would have done if you hadn't stopped by here when you did. You were truly a Godsend, Jim. I wish you didn't have to go, but I know you must," Mary said as she handed him his saddlebags.

"Yes, I've got a long way to go and when you're new to the territory it takes a little longer to make the trip," Brent smiled.

Mary looked down at the ground for a moment and then back into Brent's eyes. He saw the question in her eyes, a question he alone had the answer to.

"Is something wrong, Mary?" Brent asked.

"No, well...yes, I guess there is," she said and paused before going on. "I found the...wanted poster you had stuck in your shirt pocket when I went to wash it yesterday," she said.

Brent laughed, "Oh, and you thought that...," Brent started to say, but stopped.

If he told her he was not the man on the wanted poster she had found it might work against him. All Brent knew about the man on the poster was that he had shot him in the face with a shotgun and switched identities with him, so to speak, when he made his escape from the jail cell in Knox's Corner.

"Mary, I didn't do any of the things on that poster. It's an old one and I ran across it and took it with me. There might be some people around that don't know the poster is no longer any good," Brent said, stretching the truth somewhat.

"Well, all I know is that we don't know the man described in this poster. You more than likely saved our lives; at least some of us," she said with a smile.

Just about then Luke ran out with the biscuits, followed by his brother Ben. The two of them had taken a strong liking to Brent; or Jim Jones as he had introduced himself to them.

Brent looked around to make sure he had all his belongings and then mounted up. He stuck the wrapped biscuits inside his shirt. They were still warm and since the morning was a bit cool they felt good against his skin.

"I wish you could wait until Steve gets back from the feed store. I'm sure he'd want to tell you goodbye," Mary said.

"We said our goodbyes when he pulled out. You folks take good care of yourselves and Luke, you and Ben mind your ma and pa. They're good people," Brent said as he reined his horse around to head north.

"We will, Jim. Don't forget to come back. You said you would," Luke called after him.

"Good luck Jim," Mary said and then added, "May God go with you."

"Thank you Mary. Adios," Brent said and kicked the spirited palomino into an easy lope.

US Marshal Earl Haddock sat in the only general store in the small settlement of Knox's Corner with a deep frown etched on his face. He had talked to the two Texas Rangers who had arrested Brent Sackett and left him locked up in a makeshift jail there in Knox's Corner.

When Haddock arrived to pick Sackett up, however, he was told that Sackett had been shot in the face with a shotgun after having killed the town's constable while trying to escape. The man who had shot Sackett had ridden away and no one knew who he was, where he came from or where he was headed when he rode off.

"Would you like another cup of coffee, Earl?" the store owner asked the marshal.

"No, thanks just the same. So...you have no idea who the hombre was who shot this Sackett and then just rode away, huh?" Haddock asked.

"Nope, I'd never seen him before. I can tell you one thing though. He was riding one of the most beautiful animals I've ever seen. A golden palomino stud that looked like it could run all day and all night and still not be winded," the owner of the store said.

"Well, I guess there's nothing for me to do then. If those two Texas Rangers pass through here again tell them what you told me, will you? That should close the book on this Brent Sackett. I'd sure like to know more about this man who shot him, though," the marshal said thoughtfully.

"If I see them I'll be sure and relay the message. I'll put the word out to the other folks around here to do the same. You know, just in case they see the rangers and I don't," the owner said.

"Well, I'd better get along. I've got to make a trip up to Sacramento in a few days and I've got a number of things to take care of in preparation for my journey. Thanks for the coffee," the marshal said as he got up to leave.

"We heard there was a bank robbery up north a few days ago. Do you have any leads on the men who did it?" the owner asked.

"We got one of the men, but the rest of the gang got away. From what we know there were five men who participated in the holdup," the marshal said and then paused as his eyes widened.

"You did say the man who shot Sackett was riding a palomino, didn't you? We were told that one of the men was riding a beautiful palomino."

"Yes I did say that. One of the most beautiful animals I've seen in a long while. Do you think he might be one of the gang?"

"He just might be. Thanks for the information. At least we know that there's the possibility they're still in the area," the marshal said and then added. "Well, I gotta get a move on. Thanks again for everything. Have a good day," the marshal said and went out to where his horse was tied.

He mounted up and gave the store owner, who had walked out onto the store's front porch a final wave. He headed his horse in the direction of San Diego, or Old Town as it was referred to, where his office was located.

Marshal Haddock didn't know it, but one day in the near future he would have a face to face encounter with the man he thought was dead...Brent Sackett.

Chapter 2

Knox's Corner
October 31, 1879

The two wagons pulled to a stop and Grant Holt called out to Cheryl Keeling, "Let's give the horses a breather. I think we can all use a little rest. We've got another five hours of daylight so no need to push the horses any harder than necessary."

"Yeah, I think we have a couple of young ones who can use a 'potty break'," Cheryl laughed.

The kids, Hank and Annie Thurston, jumped down off the wagon and headed for some underbrush. Cheryl checked on Grant's baby and once she was satisfied the baby was okay, she walked to a small brook that was about forty yards away.

Cheryl dipped a handkerchief into the cool water and wiped her face. She closed her eyes as she felt the water run down her face and onto her neck. She dipped the handkerchief into the water again and this time ran if across the back of her neck.

The sound of a covey of quail flying caused her to look in the direction of the noise. Something had frightened the birds, but what? Just then Hank Thurston, followed by his little sister Annie, made their way to where Cheryl was seated.

"Oh, this is a nice spot don't you think, Mrs. Keeling?" Hank said. "Look how good the ground is around here. I'll bet you could grow just about anything in this land."

Cheryl couldn't hold back the smile as she said, "Yes and isn't this the best little pond you've ever seen."

"Uh huh," Hank grinned. "It sure would make a good swimming hole during the summertime," he answered.

Annie, Hank's little sister was busy picking wild flowers when suddenly she called out, "Hank, Mrs. Keeling...look at this."

Cheryl and Hank walked over to the small tree where Annie was standing and looked down at the base of it. A bag of money had been buried at the base of the tree, but a coyote or some other wild animal had managed to dig it up.

"Oh my goodness," Cheryl said, "Now how do you suppose this got buried there?" she wondered as she picked up the bag.

"I don't know," Hank said and then asked, "How much do you think is there?"

Cheryl made a quick count and said, "There's over a thousand dollars here, Hank. Quick, go get Grant and Daysha."

Daysha Jones, who had joined up with the two wagons in Yuma, and Grant were back with the wagons as Hank took off running in that direction. When he reached them he blurted out, "Annie just found a sack full of money. Come see."

The three of them ran back to where Mrs. Keeling was and stopped when she held up the money Annie had found.

Grant looked at the money and then at Cheryl, "Did you count it?"

"Yes, there's one thousand two hundred and twelve dollars here. This is the bag it was in when Annie found it. It looks like someone buried the money and then wild animals dug it up. Do you think the money might be stolen?" Cheryl asked.

"It's hard to say; it is in a bag the bank might use. Maybe someone was afraid of being held up and buried the money to keep bandits from getting their hands on it," Grant said.

"What are you going to do with it?" Daysha asked.

"I don't know. If we turn it over to the nearest sheriff he could say he never got it and even get a posse after us. If we don't do anything, and it is stolen, we could be arrested for having stolen money in our possession," Grant said and then slowly shook his head negatively. "I wish Brent was here. He'd know what to do."

"Think like Brent, then. What would he do?" Mrs. Keeling said thoughtfully.

Hank Thurston spoke up, "He'd say, 'We'll hold onto it and see what happens. If nothing happens and no one comes looking for it, then it was meant for us to have the money. If someone does come looking for it and they're good people...we give it to 'em."

Cheryl smiled as she thought how right Hank just might be, "Okay, then that's what we'll do. First we'll take it out of the bag and put it in one of the wagons for safe keeping," Cheryl added.

"Can I have the bag?" Annie Thurston asked. "I can make a dress out of it for my doll."

"Sure thing, honey," Cheryl said with a warm smile.

They had no way of knowing that the money they had just found had been stolen by a man Brent had been forced to kill a few days earlier. But something that is found has a history and that history can sometimes be connected to something very evil; especially when the thing found is stolen money.

At that very moment there were three men on the trail of the man Brent Sackett had killed while making his escape from jail. One of the men was the dead man's brother; the other two were the remaining members of the gang.

"Where's that brother of yours, Ben? We laid it out that if we got separated we'd meet back here. I see us, but no Jess," Will Culhane said with a frown.

"I asked Jess if he understood the plan and he said he did. You know how easily he gets confused, though," Ben Hooker said with a frown.

"That's what he *said*, Ben. But, look around and tell me where you see him at. I'm looking and I don't see him. He may be your brother, but he's as loco as an Injun on peyote. How'd he wind up with the money, anyway?" Will Culhane asked angrily.

"When Sam went down Jess picked up the saddlebags as he ran by him," Ben replied.

"He shouldn't be too hard to track down; not riding that palomino of his. We can't hang around here waiting for him, though. He's got that money and I want it. I say we start backtracking and see if we can't run across his trail," Culhane said disgustedly.

"That's a might risky, don't you think, Will?" Hutch Bolen asked.

"Yeah, maybe it is, Hutch, but I'm not going to just give up on finding Jess and our money. Besides, we wore masks and I doubt anyone could identify us. Jess has more to worry about on that count than we do. That horse of his stands out head and shoulders over most horses," Culhane replied.

"It does at that," Hutch answered and then had a thought. "Say, I recall the conversation I had with Jess not long before we entered that bank. He said something that caused me to wonder if he might be a little confused about our meeting place if we got separated."

"What'd he say?" Culhane asked.

"He said he knew the perfect spot to 'bury' the money. It was Knox's Corner. When I asked him about it later, though, he couldn't remember what he'd said about it," Hutch replied.

"That's Jess alright. He's loco like I said. Well, who knows…maybe he remembered what he'd told you and that's where he headed. I guess it's worth a look see. Come on let's ride. We can be there in a couple hours," Culhane said and reined his horse in the direction of Knox's Corner.

Cheryl had just finished fixing a hot meal for everyone as Grant led the horses back from the well where he'd watered them. Daysha was busy with Grant's baby daughter. She was beginning to feel like she was really the baby's mother.

"Come and get it," Cheryl called out.

Everyone quickly finished up what they were doing quickly and came to the campfire for their supper. They had just sat down and begun to eat when the three members of the Culhane gang rode up to their campsite.

Grant got up and greeted the men, placing his hand on the gun he was wearing.

"Howdy," Grant said as he studied the men carefully. He didn't have a good feeling about them.

"Howdy...we smelled your food cooking and thought you might spare some of it. We've been in the saddle all day and are bone weary," Culhane said with a bent grin.

"Cheryl, do we have any extra food tonight?" Grant called to Cheryl.

"We've got a little extra. I guess we can feed three more," Cheryl said realizing the men could see the kettle over the open fire.

"Step down, men. We've been invited to supper," Culhane said as he climbed out of the saddle.

The three men walked over to the campfire and helped themselves to the stew. Not one of them showed any real gratitude, but merely started eating as if they hadn't eaten for days.

They didn't say a word until they had wiped up the last of their food with the bread Cheryl had given them. That's when Culhane looked at Cheryl with dead eyes and said, "You got any coffee?"

"Yeah, right there in the pot; help your self," Cheryl said in a cool tone of voice.

Culhane grabbed a tin cup and poured himself a cup of coffee. The other two did likewise. They sat back down and Culhane looked carefully at Cheryl, then Grant and Daysha, and last at Hank and Annie Thurston.

"So where are you folks bound for?" Culhane asked.

"The Sacramento area," Grant said, although Culhane continued to stare at Cheryl.

"Sacramento, eh...you're a little far from the beaten trail to be headed that way," Culhane grinned.

"We came from Yuma," Daysha interjected warily.

"So, are you two married?" Culhane asked, looking from Cheryl to Grant.

"No, I'm married to her," Grant said pointing to Daysha who moved closer to Grant.

Culhane looked at Cheryl and said, "Where's your man?"

"He went ahead to check out the best way to go from here," Cheryl said, sensing danger.

"You folks didn't happen to see a man traveling by himself and riding a palomino did you?" Culhane asked.

"We haven't seen anyone for over a day and a half," Grant said.

"We're supposed to meet our man here. When are you folks moving on?" Culhane asked.

"In the morning...early," Grant said firmly.

Hank Thurston had been eyeing the three men and didn't have a good feeling about them either. There was something about the way they kept looking around the campsite as though searching for something.

Hank got up and moved to the back of the wagon. When no one was looking he climbed into the wagon and got the pistol that Brent had left for them and had shown Hank where he was leaving it.

Brent didn't want to go off and leave them without enough firepower to protect themselves should the need arrive. Hank felt they might have need of the gun very shortly.

Hank laid the pistol at the back of the wagon so it would be within easy reach should he need to get to it quickly. He climbed out of the wagon but remained at the back of the wagon so the gun was within easy reach. He stood there and watched the men very closely.

Annie walked back to where Hank was standing and grabbed her doll out of the back of the wagon. Annie had made a dress for her doll out of the bank's money bag they'd found.

Hank didn't notice Annie taking the doll until she had reentered the campsite and sat down next to Daysha. No one paid any attention to Annie at first but after several seconds Ben Hooker glanced at the doll in Annie's hand and then looked away.

It suddenly dawned on him what he'd just seen and he did a double take, this time staring hard at the doll's dress. He wasted no time in grabbing the doll and saying to Annie, "Where'd you get this dress your doll's wearing?"

His sudden rant scared Annie and she clutched the doll to her chest. Daysha jumped to her feet and grabbed Annie, quickly hugging the child to her bosom and snapped angrily, "Don't talk to her like that."

Hooker grabbed the doll away from Annie and said to Culhane, "This is the moneybag from the bank."

"So it is," Culhane said and took the bag from Hooker.

Looking at Grant he snapped, "Where'd you get this bag?"

"We found it over by a tree near here. Why? What's so important about an old bag?" Grant said in an innocent tone of voice.

"What was in it?" Culhane demanded as he drew his pistol.

"Nothing was in it, it was just a bag over by that tree there," Grant said.

Daysha led Annie over to where Cheryl was standing and then moved away from the two of them in preparation for what was about to happen.

When Culhane looked in the direction Grant had pointed, Grant went for his gun. Hooker had glanced off as well as Culhane, but looked back at Grant as he was going for the gun on his hip.

"Watch it," Hooker yelled just as Grant fired at Culhane.

21

Grant's bullet hit Culhane in the chest knocking him to the ground. Hooker had pulled his gun, but before he could fire another shot rang out from the back of the wagon; it was fired by Hank Thurston.

Hank's bullet hit Hooker in the side. Staggering backwards Hooker fired a shot into the ground. Another shot rang out from Hutch Bolen's gun, the bullet hitting Grant in the shoulder. Before Hutch could fire again there was a 'pop' sound that produced a bullet hole directly between the bandit's eyes.

Daysha had pulled a Derringer from the small ankle holster she wore and shot Hutch Bolen dead. Cheryl looked on in stunned silence as she held little Annie close to her.

Daysha looked down at the man she'd just shot with eyes wide. Her hand began to shake slightly and she dropped the Derringer from her hand and looked quickly at Cheryl.

"I've never shot anyone before, Cheryl. Oh my God, what have I done?" Daysha said solemnly.

"You probably saved at least one of our lives, maybe more than that. They would have killed us Daysha, believe me. These were not upstanding citizens here. There's no telling how many men the one you shot has murdered," Cheryl said in a comforting tone of voice.

"I still don't like the feeling," Daysha said.

Hank Thurston was having his own issue of shooting someone. He had dropped the gun he'd used also and was staring down at the dead man. Grant noticed how Hank was reacting to the shooting and quickly tried to console the young boy.

"Hank, you just did a brave thing. I don't mean the shooting of the man; I mean protecting your little sister the way you did. That took courage and you stood up against some very bad men. I don't want you to carry this around with you. It isn't something you ever want to do again, but you had to do it this time," Grant said putting his arm around Hank's shoulder.

"I hope I never have to do it again, Grant. This is something I'll be thinking about for a long, long time," Hank said seriously.

"Me too, Hank...me too," Grant said.

Raymond D. Mason

Chapter 3

**Train bound for
Wichita, Kansas
November 1, 1879**

Brian Sackett watched the two men seated near the back of the railroad car without their being aware of it. They had been asking a number of questions about the train's schedule which had aroused the conductor's suspicions a bit and he had informed the two railroad detectives of this.

After observing the men for several minutes 'Big Mike' McManus told Sackett they should move closer to the men where they might hear some of their conversation. McManus made the first move and pretended to be looking for someone aboard the train.

Once he got behind the two men he sat down and waited for Sackett to join him. Brian made a show of recognizing his partner and approached him with a smile.

"Oh, there you are Mike. I just checked on that bull we have in the cattle car; he's doing fine,"

Brian said loud enough for the two men seated in front of McManus would hear.

McManus couldn't hold back a grin knowing what Brian was up to. The two men gave the tall man a quick glance and went back to their subdued conversation.

Brian sat down next to Big Mike and got a slight head nod of approval by the seasoned railroad detective along with the smile. McManus then noticed something else which caused the smile to drop. It was two men who entered the car at the far end.

Brian noticed the change of demeanor in McManus and turned his attention towards the two men who had just entered the car.

"We've got trouble," McManus whispered. "The two men who just entered the car are Ben Horner and Will Ballard. They're suspected of hitting one of our trains before."

Brian eyed the two new arrivals and caught the slight glance they gave the two men seated in front of him and McManus. It was fairly obvious to even a new man like Sackett that these four men knew one another and were either planning a robbery or was about to try and pull one off.

McManus had informed Sackett that the mail car was carrying over ten thousand dollars in cash and would be a good score for any would be train robbers. It looked like Horner, Ballard and the two men in front of them were about to try and rob the train.

Brian saw McManus slowly draw his revolver from under his coat and hold it down so it was out of sight and did the same. Brian quickly deduced that Horner and Ballard would take a position at the other end of the car, which they did.

The air filled with tension as McManus and Sackett eyed the four men closely. The detectives knew the robbery was underway when the train began to slow to a stop. Someone was in the engine along with the engineer and his coal man.

McManus leaned slightly towards Sackett and whispered, "I'll take Horner and Ballard; you take these two."

Brian nodded his answer and they waited for the robbers to make the next move. They didn't have to wait long. Horner and Ballard didn't take a seat, but stood at the end of the car.

It was then that the two men nearest McManus and Sackett made their move. They stood up drawing their guns as they stood. The moment they did, McManus made his move.

"All right, everybody...," the taller of the two men yelled out, but before he could finish his order, McManus gave him a shove forward and fired at Horner, hitting him in the shoulder.

Brian instantly hit the man nearest him over the head with his gun, knocking the man out cold. The man McManus had pushed caught his balance and turned, aiming his gun in the detectives' direction. Brian shot him, hitting him in the chest.

The man went down next to the man Brian had pistol whipped; only he was dead while the other man was merely unconscious. McManus fired at Ballard, but the outlaw had ducked down between two seats with train passengers directly in front of him.

Women began screaming while the men grabbed the ladies and pulled them down out of harms way. Ballard fired at McManus over the heads of the passengers in front of him.

Brian didn't hesitate. He ran out the exit nearest him and McManus onto the small platform at the back of the car. From there he quickly scampered up a ladder that led to the top of the passenger car.

When Brian bolted for the door, McManus turned and saw his assistant leaving him to face Ballard alone. He frowned deeply as he muttered, "Thanks a lot, Sackett."

Brian moved carefully along the roof of the passenger car as he made his way to the opposite end and climbed down the ladder located there. The gunfire was still erupting inside the car and he knew he would have to hurry.

Once on the car landing he carefully opened the door just a crack in order to look inside. He couldn't see Ballard, but knew exactly where he was due to the gunfire.

When McManus saw Brian peer through the slightly opened door he held off on his gunfire. Ballard, thinking the detective was reloading, used the moment to make what he thought was his escape. What he did was rush out the door straight into Sackett who hit him with a crushing right hand to the chin and knocked him out with one punch.

The attempted train robbery had been brought to an abrupt end. McManus ran to where Brian was, but only after having handcuffed the first man Sackett had cold cocked.

As McManus moved towards Brian he held his gun on Horner who was seated and holding his badly wounded shoulder. The pain had been too much for Horner to continue firing. All he could do now was swear at McManus for wounding him.

"I'll take care of the man in the engine," Brian said as he bolted out of the car and ran towards the front of the train. When he got there the engineer pointed to a thicket and yelled out, "He ran in there."

Brian eyed the thicket and started moving cautiously towards it. Before he got to it, however, he heard the sound of hoof beats on the far side of the underbrush. He climbed up on the steps of the engine for a better view.

He saw two riders making tracks away from the train. When one of the men looked back towards the train, Brian noticed the patch over the man's right eye. He couldn't be sure, but a name shot through his mind like a bolt of lightning. The name was Cable Dutton; a man who had sworn to kill him for costing him the sight in his right eye.

Brian returned to the car where McManus was holding the other train robbers. When he walked in the passengers looked at him and several broke into applause. Of course, they were the ones who were carrying the most money on their person.

"Good work, Sackett. When you split for the door back there, I thought you were leaving me to fend for myself," McManus said with a wide grin.

"I thought you might think that," Brian grinned and then added. "The one up front in the engine got away. There was another man holding their horses behind a thicket. They were too far away for me to get a shot at them with this handgun."

"They must have heard all the shooting," McManus replied.

"Shooting always sends a message and puts bad men on the run," Brian grinned.

Mc Manus looked at Brian approvingly and said, "I'll let you cuff this one. Then we'll move them to the mail car and give them a good look at the car they wanted to rob. That'll be as close to the money as they'll ever get," McManus said with a laugh.

Meanwhile, Cable Dutton and the man who had managed to escape from the train with him, reined up in a draw. Dutton climbed down off his horse and sat down on the ground. He pulled a plug of tobacco from his pocket and took a chaw of it.

"Here, Keno" Dutton said and tossed the plug of chewing tobacco to him. Keno bit off a chaw and tossed it back.

"Who were those two, do you know?" Keno asked?

"I'm not sure of the one man, but the tall one I could swear was a man named Sackett, Brian Sackett. He's the one who left me with this," Dutton said motioning towards his eye patch.

"Do you think they work for the railroad?" Keno continued to question.

"I don't know, Keno. The last I heard Sackett was down in Texas working on the family ranch. I had always planned on making a trip down there to even the score for my eye," Dutton said.

"If you got that good a look at him, then he must have gotten a pretty good look at you, too. Maybe we ought to clear out of these parts," Keno went on.

"If that hombre was Sackett I won't leave here until I see him dead," Dutton snapped angrily.

"How are you going to do that if they post your picture all over the state?"

"Haven't you ever heard of a disguise? I'll just change my looks some, that's all."

"Yeah, like chop yourself down to about six feet four, huh? How are you going to alter the fact that you're pushing six feet eight?" Keno asked.

"There're other things I can do, like shave off this beard for one. I just want to get close enough to get my hands on him, or put a bullet in him."

"I'd stick with the gun. He's already cost you one eye," Keno said raising Dutton's ire.

Dutton reached out and slapped Keno's face hard. Keno bristled and started to go for his gun, but then backed off when Dutton spoke.

"Go for it and you'll die right here," Dutton said with a growl more than a voice.

"Don't ever hit me again, Dutton. Next time and I will go for my gun."

"Next time I won't use the back of my hand," Dutton responded.

Raymond D. Mason

Chapter 4

Point of Rocks
Cimarron Grassland
November 2, 1879

Bounty hunter, Shell Sackett was taking Don Stratton back to Santa Fe, New Mexico to stand trial for robbing the stagecoach that Shell's fiancé had been a passenger on. She had been killed by Stratton and Sackett had been on his trail for months, finally catching up to him in Dodge City, Kansas.

Along on the trip were two other men; Quirt Adams and Bill Bell. They had teamed up with Sackett in Dodge City and were going to ride with him part of the way.

Quirt Adams led the foursome having traveled that stretch several times. They hadn't seen another living soul for several days, but that was about to change.

The traveling was very easy through this part of the Cimarron territory with a few gently rolling hills, wooded areas, plenty of good water and grazing. The Beaty brothers upon seeing this area that same year had just established the Point of Rocks Ranch.

Quirt Adams eyed the area with the business eye of a cattleman, while Bell saw it as merely some pretty scenery. Sackett saw it as a part of the Santa Fe Trail and Stratton saw it as a good place to plan his escape.

Stratton eyed the rocky crag as a good place to use as an escape route if he could commandeer one of the guns of his captors. He looked closely at every draw, every tree; every avenue he could use to escape the men taking him to Santa Fe.

He made up his mind that this would be the place he bolted. The timing would have to be just right and he knew it. The problem was that all three men were very savvy when it came to handling a prisoner. He'd have to make an excuse to get alone with one of the men. The most likely one would be Bell, since he knew very little about him and he was closer in size to him than the other two men.

Stratton called out to the others asking if they could take a breather. Sackett was the only one to answer him and did so bluntly, "No!"

Stratton grinned ever so slightly and complained mildly, "Hey, I'd like to relieve myself, Sackett. I don't think you want me doing that from horseback, do you?"

Sackett took a deep breath and let it out in a rush, "Okay, okay," he said and called out to Quirt. "Hey Quirt, let's take a five minute breather."

"Sure thing, this is a good spot with the river right there," Quirt said.

He started to rein up when he saw several riders just topping a slight rise. He counted three, but then a fourth took up the rear. Quirt called back to the others.

"We've got company. Looks like four riders...they're white, if that makes any difference."

"I don't like to see over two men riding together," Sackett said.

"I don't either," Bell agreed.

"Me neither," Stratton said.

"Who asked you," Sackett snapped back.

"I just thought you'd be interested in my thoughts on the subject," Stratton answered.

"Well, I'm not interested in anything you might think," Sackett said without the least bit of a smile.

Stratton figured if he could lay his hands on a gun, Shell Sackett would be the first man he gunned down. His scowl at Sackett didn't go unnoticed by Bill Bell who commented, "I don't think Stratton likes you very much, Shell."

"Good, cause I sure don't like him," Shell replied quickly.

The four riders reined up about ten feet short of where Quirt was seated on his horse with one leg thrown over the saddle horn. This indicated he considered the men friendly. He rested his right hand on his pistol, however, should he need it.

"Howdy, men," the lead rider said.

"Howdy, how're you boys doing?" Quirt asked.

"Fine, fine," the lead rider of the four said. "Where are you headed?"

Quirt glanced back at the others and stated, "Santa Fe, New Mexico."

"Oh, then I guess you wouldn't be thinking about staying in this area?" the leader said.

"Nope, we sure ain't. I've got a ranch down in Arizona that requires all the work, blood, sweat and tears I can muster now," Quirt said.

"Oh, a cattleman, eh?" the man asked.

"Yep, I've got a good sized spread. We run anywhere from 20-25 thousand head."

"Sounds like a good operation," the spokesman said just as Bill Bell rode up alongside Quirt leaving Shell Sackett with the prisoner.

"Do these men work for you?" the lead rider asked.

"No, actually we're taking a prisoner down to Santa Fe to stand trial for murder and robbery," Quirt stated.

The four riders glanced in Stratton's direction and the spokesman said, "The one in the iron bracelets I take it?"

"No, he's the lawman; it's the one next to him that's the bad guy," Quirt said as a joke.

The men looked at him seriously for a moment and then all of them burst into laughter.

"I guess that was a cockeyed thing to say on my part," the rider said.

"I couldn't resist the 'rib'," Quirt said and then added. "Oh, my name is Quirt Adams and this is Bill Bell," Quirt said extending a hand towards Bell.

"I'm Bob Beaty and these are my brothers. I just want you men to feel free to cross our ranchland and use all the wood and water you might need," the spokesman said.

"Thank you...I doubt we'll use much of anything, though, seeing as how we're just passing through," Quirt said.

Shell Sackett had moved his horse a might closer in order to hear most of what was being said. As he did so, it allowed Stratton to back his horse up slightly so he could actually reach the saddle scabbard on Sackett's mount.

He knew he would be hindered by the handcuffs but he felt this was the best chance he might have to attempt his escape. Stratton quickly formulated a plan of escape; now if he could just pull it off.

"Say, Sackett...I need to go behind those trees over there. How about taking these cuffs off me," Stratton asked.

Sackett thought for a second and then nodded his head in agreement, but with a warning.

"Don't do anything stupid, Stratton. I don't want to kill you, but I will if need be," Sackett said evenly.

"I hear that," Stratton said and held his hands out for Sackett to unlock the cuffs.

Sackett had to lean out of the saddle to reach Stratton, which put him in an awkward position. The moment the cuffs snapped open Stratton grabbed Sackett's wrist and gave a hard yank which caused Shell to fall from his mount.

Stratton then grabbed the rifle from Sackett's saddle scabbard and reined his horse around, knocking Sackett down in the process. He kicked it into a full gallop in the direction of a large rock formation.

Finally getting his feet under him, Sackett spun around as he drew out his pistol. He fired but the bullet missed the fleeing Stratton. He fired again, but Stratton had already pulled out of pistol range.

Bell instantly spurred his horse and gave chase. Quirt remained with the Beaty boys as Shell quickly gathered himself and swung into the saddle and followed after Stratton and Bell.

Being closer to Stratton, Bell raised his pistol and squeezed off a round. The bullet winged Stratton, but not enough to slow him down any. Sackett called out to Bell, "Don't kill him, Bill; I want him alive."

The horse Stratton was riding was fast, faster than any of the other three horses. Stratton pulled further ahead of his two pursuers with each stride of his spirited steed. He knew, however, he'd have to stop eventually and make a stand.

He rode to the top of a rocky crag and reined his horse to a halt. He leaped off the horse and knelt down behind a rock. From here he would be able to pick off the first man to top the hill. He figured it would be Bill Bell since he had been the closest one pursuing him.

When a rider-less horse appeared Stratton's eyes widened in fear. His pursuers were coming at him on foot and could show up anywhere. He looked around frantically for any sign of the three escorting him back to Santa Fe.

He cocked the hammer back on the rifle and moved to a higher point on the rocky crag. If he could just get a shot at one of the men it would make the odds a little more even. He moved to the edge of a rock that would give him a good view of the terrain below him. It was a bad mistake on his part.

Standing on the highest point above Stratton's position, Shell Sackett could see most of the rocky terrain below him. It wasn't until Stratton moved out towards the edge of the rock he was on, however, that Sackett got a good view of him.

"Hold it right there, Stratton," Sackett called out.

Stratton froze for a split second before spinning around and turning the rifle skyward. It was a mistake that would cost him his life.

The gun in Sackett's hand barked and the bullet hit Stratton in the chest. He dropped the rifle he was holding and looked down at the hole in his shirt. He looked up towards Sackett and slowly crumpled to his knees.

"I'm...I'm...dying," Stratton managed to say and then fell face down on the ground. He died the way he had lived, violently.

Sackett made his way off the rocky point to the ledge where Stratton lay. He looked down at the man and slowly shook his head.

"I didn't want to kill you outright, Stratton. I wanted to see you squirm for awhile. I wanted to see you sweat out a trial and hear the guilty call. Then I wanted to watch your face when the judge said, 'I sentence you to be hanged by the neck until you are dead.' That's what I wanted for you Stratton.

"Now, of course, you'll have to face the Judge of judges. One who will judge your soul and your motives for the things you have done in this life. His judgment will be an everlasting one. There'll be no chance for a reprieve once sentence has been passed on you by our eternal Judge," Sackett said.

Just then Bill Bell called out to him, "Are you all right, Sackett?"

"Yeah, Bill, I am. Stratton is dead though. I guess you boys can go anyway you want to now," Sackett replied.

Bill Bell made his way to where Sackett was and the two of them carried Stratton's dead body down off the rocky ledge to where his horse had stopped to graze. They tied Stratton's body across the saddle and covered it with a piece of canvas that Sackett carried with him.

They started out again, but with Stratton dead their plans changed. Quirt decided to veer to the west and visit an old friend of his he hadn't see in several years.

Bell decided to go to Amarillo, Texas therefore would be heading to the southeast. They said their goodbyes and each man took a different trail. Sackett continued on his way back to Santa Fe with Stratton's body tied across the dead man's saddle.

Chapter 5

Flagstaff, Arizona
November 2, 1979

Linc Sackett and Clay Butler walked out of the office at the train depot and stopped on the loading platform. Neither man said a word for a few seconds then both started to speak at the same time.

"He took off with...," Linc started to say, but stopped when he heard Butler starting to speak.

"Bateman caught the...," Butler said, but he too stopped when he heard Sackett speak.

They both looked at one another and Linc said, "Go ahead, what were you going to say?"

"No, you go first," Butler said.

"Bateman took off with the money all right and headed back east with it," Linc said.

"That's what I was going to say," Butler said.

"This ain't going to set well with Miss Bell, I can tell you that," Linc added.

"He planned this thing out pretty well, I'd say. The two of them get the business up and running and making good money. He suggests they open another saloon up here in Flagstaff and then splits with all the money. There's no telling how long he'd been planning this," Butler stated.

"Crooked minds work that way. He may have come up with the plan on the spur of the moment. He may have just seen an opportunity and taken it," Linc replied.

Butler thought for a moment and then asked, "If he wasn't planning on going back to Tucson why would he tell her when he was supposed to arrive there?"

"Hey, it gave him that much of a head start and made better cover for him. Crystal wouldn't have any concern until the day he was supposed to show up, but didn't. By the time she realized he wasn't coming back he could be long gone," Linc answered back.

"So what do we do? We can't really go traipsing all over the country searching for the guy. Who knows, he may change his name and how would we find him then?" Butler said thoughtfully.

"He probably will change his name. He'll know that Crystal will have the law on his trail. One thing we can do is keep our eyes peeled and if we ever run across him again grab him and turn him over to the law," Linc said.

The two of them walked down the steps of the platform to where their horses were tied and mounted up. It would be a long ride back to Tucson with nothing but bad news for Miss Crystal Bell.

Before heading back to Tucson, however, they decided to stop in at one of the local saloons and have a beer for the trail. There was a saloon not two hundred and fifty yards from the train station.

They pushed the swinging doors of the saloon open and walked into the small barroom. There were eight or nine men and three saloon gals in the bar all of whom gave the two new arrivals a casual glance.

Linc spotted an empty table at the back of the saloon right next to a poker table that was seeing action. He pointed towards the table and he and Butler headed in that direction. Just as they were nearing the table, however, Butler glanced towards the poker table and stopped short.

Sitting there at the table was none other than Lawrence Bateman. Butler looked from Bateman to Linc and gave a head nod in the gambler's direction. Linc looked that way and his eyes widened.

"Well, I'll be. I thought he bought a ticket back east?" Linc said under his breath.

The two cowboys moved up to the poker table, one standing on either side of Bateman. Bateman glanced up at Linc who was standing on his left side and then quickly looked to his right at Butler.

"Howdy, Larry," Linc said.

"How've you been?" Butler then asked.

Bateman snapped his head from side to side and then smiled widely.

"Well, hi guys. What brings you up here to Flagstaff?" Bateman asked nervously.

"Let's see...it might be $11,000 that you took out of the bank down in Tucson that belonged to you and your partner, Miss Crystal Bell," Linc stated seriously.

"Oh...I can explain that. I got up here and heard of a better deal in Winslow. Then I got in this poker game and we've been in it for two days now," Bateman said.

"Is that right?" Linc said and added, "Then how is it you bought a ticket to St. Louis, Missouri? That's a little beyond Winslow ain't it?"

"I had to buy the ticket because that's where the owner lives...in St. Louis," Bateman said as easy as if he was telling the truth.

"I'll tell you what...you have a little lady down in Tucson who thinks you've cheated her out of her hard earned money. So we'll escort you back down there and you can explain all this to her in your own words," Linc said and paused for a moment before continuing. "If you don't we're going to break both of your legs and arms along with your fingers and thumbs. How do you like that?"

Bateman looked from one man to the next and then said, "You make a strong argument for going back with you. I don't think Crystal will be quite as thrilled to have me back with her after she hears what I have to say."

"We'll let her be the judge of that. Now come on. We've got a long ride back to Tucson," Clay said.

Bateman looked at the other men in the card game as he stood up to leave. He slowly shook his head as he picked up the money in front of him.

"Well, gentlemen, it looks like I'm out of the game. I'll have to take my winnings...your money...and go with these two. Thank you for the pleasure of your company," Bateman said with a smile.

"You've got over three hundred dollars of mine. I'd like a chance to get some of it back," one of the men stated.

"He's got over two hundred and fifty of mine. I want a chance to recoup some of mine, too," another man said.

The third man in the five man poker game nodded his head in agreement, but merely said, "Me too." The fourth man didn't say anything because he was money ahead along with Bateman.

"I'll tell you what we'll do, gentlemen," Linc said. "We'll stay here over night and leave in the morning. You'll have the rest of the day and tonight to try to get your money back. He leaves at 8 o'clock tomorrow morning, though, whether you've got your money back or not."

"Fair enough," the men agreed.

Linc and Butler took a table across from the poker table so they could keep an eye on Bateman. They set up a system for how they would keep him in sight until they left. It was agreed that they would take turns watching him.

The first one to keep watch over the gambler was Linc. Clay Butler went down the street and got a hotel room for them so they would be well rested when 8 o'clock the next morning rolled around.

Meanwhile, Lawrence Bateman sat in the poker game with two things on his mind. The first was the game itself, and the second was how he could get away from Sackett and Butler. There was no way he wanted to make a return trip to Tucson.

By the time Linc and Butler traded shifts at keeping an eye on Bateman, the gambler had hatched an idea for slipping away from the two.

He'd need a little help in doing so, but he had gotten friendly with one of the saloon gals who would probably be willing to help.

Bateman won a couple of hands and waved for the gal he'd been friendly with to come over and take an order for a round of drinks.

"This round is on me, gentlemen. I figure it's the least I can do seeing as how I'm taking your hard earned money from you," he said with a grin.

As the woman neared, Bateman smiled and said, "Honey bring each man here a drink of their choice, and that fella sitting over there, take a glass of your finest Brandy and make it a double," he said motioning towards Butler.

He gave the girl a wink and a head nod in Butler's direction and said, "Keep a glass in his hand, honey."

He hoped she would catch on that he wanted to get Butler drunk so he could make his getaway. She got Bateman's drift and nodded back. Bateman handed her a twenty dollar bill and whispered, "There'll be more later."

After several more drinks Bateman could tell that Butler was beginning to feel the effects of the strong drinks. Keeping a sharp eye on Butler, Bateman's anticipation of making a getaway heightened as he watched the man's eyes begin to droop.

It wasn't long before Butler had relaxed to a point of dozing off. Bateman waited until he was sure Butler was asleep and excused himself from the game to visit the privy.

Butler suddenly snapped his eyes open and looked at the poker table. When he saw Bateman was gone he jumped to his feet and asked, "Where's the man who was sitting there?"

"He had to go outback, but he said he'd be right back," one of the men at the table said.

"Oh great," Butler said as he jumped up and headed for the back door.

Linc Sackett frowned as he listened to Clay's explanation of what happened. When Clay had finished his confession Linc shook his head and took a deep breath.

"Well, partner, he won't be as easy to find now. He knows we're on his trail and he'll be as wily as a coyote from here on out. I hate to do it to Crystal, but I think about all we can do now is go back to Tucson with the bad news," Linc said.

"I feel bad about this, Linc. Maybe I ought to stay on Bateman's trail and follow him around until I catch up to him. What do you think?" Butler asked.

"That's up to you. I could run the show while you're gone, I guess. Do what you think is right. That decision, though will be entirely yours," Linc said honestly.

Clay thought about it for a moment and then said, "I lost him; I'll find him."

"Okay, that settles it then," Linc said and then added. "I'll head back to Tucson with the news. Check back there from time to time and let me know where you are and how I can get in touch with you if the need should arrive."

"I'll keep you posted as to where I'm headed next and I'll check with the telegraph office when I get there and just before I leave. Tell Crystal not to worry. I'll find him if it takes forever," Butler said.

"Let's not get carried away here, partner. Give it a couple of months and then head on back. I'm sure Crystal will understand."

The next morning Linc left for Tucson and Clay started his search for Lawrence Bateman. Clay's first stop was the train station and then the stagecoach depot. As an afterthought he checked at the two stables in town.

Clay learned from the stableman at the second stable he checked out that a man answering Bateman's description had been there the day before.

"Yeah, he bought a little strawberry roan mare that I had for sale. She was sound as a dollar, that little mare was...or is it, is? Anyway he bought her," the man said.

"He didn't say where he was headed, did he?" Clay asked.

"No sir, he didn't. But, I noticed he headed out of town in the direction of Russell's Tank," the man said.

Clay grinned as he figured that had to be Bateman. He'd been heading east and now he was changing direction.

"Oh, one other thing about that horse he bought. It has an odd gait that causes it to leave a definite track mark. It looks something like this," the stableman said and drew the shape in the dirt. Just after he finished he noticed one of the hoof prints the horse had made the day before. Clay was fortunate there had been no other horses disturbing the track. He wouldn't have any trouble staying on Bateman's trail now, he was sure.

Clay wasted no time in saddling up and heading to the small settlement of Russell's Tank. Butler hoped to make up some valuable ground on Bateman and hopefully could catch up with him in Russell's Tank. Clay kept his horse in a slow gallop making sure the horse never went to long without him taking a breather.

Once Clay reached the open road and passed the city limits sign there were fewer horse tracks, thereby making his job of tracking Bateman that much easier. Clay didn't realize just how dangerous a man Bateman was when cornered. He had been to prison once and swore he would never go back again.

Raymond D. Mason

Chapter 7

**Near the City of Angeles
November 3, 1879**

Brent Sackett held a steady pace as he rode along what was called El Camino Real enjoying the view and wondering how Cheryl and the others were getting along. He also thought of Julie, the woman he'd been married to for a short time. Julie had given him a few months of true love unlike anything he'd ever known. It was her love that had affected his life to a point of changing his ways.

The problem was that Julie was no longer here. He was left with just her memory and although he had loved her so much he found it hard at times to remember exactly how she looked.

He could see her well enough in his mind's eye, but as the days turned into weeks and then months, her image wasn't nearly as clear. Brent was beginning to entertain thoughts like those he had before he met and fell in love with Julie; and it bothered him.

Perhaps it was the pain of knowing true love and then losing it that had spawned these feelings of loneliness. Brent felt that nothing was forever; everything was fleeting. It was here one moment and then in the blink of an eye it was gone.

Brent got so caught up in his thoughts that he failed to notice the two riders who were coming up fast behind him. It wasn't until he heard the sound of hoof beats that he turned and saw the men approaching.

Brent figured them to be lawmen; possibly the two Texas Rangers that had arrested him earlier. He wasn't taking any chances. He reined his horse off the main road putting his heels to it and heading cross country. There was no way he could let the two men catch up to him. When he looked back he felt sure they were lawmen. They were giving chase.

Brent was thankful that it was getting late in the day, but darkness also had its drawback. The darkness might help him lose his pursuers, but not knowing the area's terrain would make it more dangerous in keeping up a rapid pace.

He had ridden about a mile and a half when he came to a creek. The water was only about a foot deep and had good flow making it impossible to tell if a horse and rider had traveled up or downstream.

Brent stayed in the creek for about a mile before it intersected another creek. He turned and rode upstream in the other creek for another half mile or so before riding out of it and taking to the hills.

Sackett's maneuver and the quickly falling darkness allowed him to lose the two lawmen who had given chase. As he reached the top of a hill he looked back towards the creek and saw the glow from two torches.

A smile spread slowly across his face as he noticed the torches were moving in the opposite direction from which he had traveled. They had lost his trail and would soon give up the chase.

He rode on over the hilltop and continued on for another couple of miles before finally stopping and giving his horse a much needed rest.

Brent dry-camped that night and was up an hour before dawn and on the trail to the northeast. It took him a good day and a half before he came to a small settlement. It turned out the settlement had no official law officers bringing a sigh of relief to Brent.

There were only three buildings in the small settlement; a blacksmith's shop, a general store and a small saloon that also served as a church on Sunday mornings. Brent stopped at all three places.

Sackett left his horse with the blacksmith to have a loose shoe replaced. He went to the bar where he was able to get something to eat; and to the general store to pick up a few supplies.

Brent returned to the blacksmith's and paid him for putting the new shoe on his horse and asked him the best route to Sacramento to avoid going through too many towns. The blacksmith was very helpful.

Just after the smithy had given him directions Brent glanced down the main road through the settlement and noticed two riders approaching. He couldn't tell if it was the two men who had been trailing him and wasn't about to take any chances that it might be them.

He thanked the blacksmith and led the palomino around to the side of the blacksmith's shop before mounting up. He headed out in the direction the blacksmith had told him was the best route to take.

The palomino had gotten its wind and was ready to run. Brent kept his eye on the trail behind him as he held the golden stallion in check. By the time he reached the first bend in the trail he had still not seen any sign of the two riders.

To be on the safe side Brent slacked the reins on the palomino stallion, but held it to a gallop. If the two riders were the law they'd more than likely stop at the blacksmith's and ask if he'd seen a rider that answered to his description.

In fact, that's exactly what the lawmen did, but it wasn't the rider they described to the smithy. They asked if a man riding a beautiful palomino stallion had passed that way.

The blacksmith, not being a fan of lawmen, told them he had seen a man riding a beautiful golden palomino. He then proceeded to send them in the opposite direction from which Brent had gone.

According to what the blacksmith had told Brent the best way to reach Sacramento was to head towards a town called Bakersfield. If he stayed close to the different mountain ranges he wouldn't have very many towns of any size to deal with.

Brent knew that he'd have to avoid the more populated settlements due to the lawmen. He feared that a description of him would be sent by telegraph to every lawman throughout California.

The further north he traveled the more he realized how accurate the blacksmith had been in his assessment of the trip. He pushed on northward in the direction of the town of Bakersfield.

Bakersfield, California
November 4, 1879

Bakersfield was a small town of just under a thousand people. It had a church, three saloons, a general store, blacksmith, Chinese laundry, a couple of cafés, feed store, land office, gunsmith, ladies and gents clothing store, a drugstore and a bank.

It was a quiet town located at the southern most end of the San Joaquin Valley. It was a town where everyone knew everyone else and cared enough to give their neighbors a helping hand when they needed it.

On the 4th of November three men entered the Cattlemen's Bank in Bakersfield while two remained outside with the horses. The men all wore rain slickers although there was not a cloud in the sky. While one of the men went up to the teller's window the other two men moved to opposite ends of the bank.

Suddenly the man standing at the teller's window yelled out loudly, "Up with your hands, this is a hold up."

The teller stepped back away from the window and raised his hands high over his head. The other teller put his hands in the air, but remained at his window. The bank president, however, went for a pistol in his desk drawer. It was a big mistake on his part.

The man at the south end of the bank raised his gun and fired once, the bullet killing the banker. The man standing at the teller's window rushed around to the swinging gate that gave him entrance to the cash boxes at the two windows and began grabbing the money and stuffing it into a bag he had with him.

Once the leader of the gang had gathered up all the bills he rushed back around towards the front door. The other two men closed in behind him, backing out of the bank holding their guns on the tellers and three customers.

The holdup men swung into the saddles and kicked their horses into a full gallop. As they rode away one of the clerks from the bank ran out and began yelling "Holdup" at the top of his lungs and brandishing a pistol. He fired three shots at the fleeing bandits, but missed badly.

Sheriff Dirk Holliman rushed out of his office as the men rounded the corner a good hundred yards down the street. Instantly he called back inside the jailhouse to his deputy, Walt Hostetter.

The two lawmen ran down the street towards the bank where a fairly large crowd was gathering. As they approached the bank they were met by the bank teller who had sounded the alarm.

"It was the Heller gang, Sheriff," the teller said.
"Are you sure?" the sheriff asked.

"I'd know Garth Heller anywhere. There isn't a mask anywhere could cover that scar across his neck," the teller replied.

"How many of you men are willing to be sworn in as posse members?" the sheriff called out.

Six men said they'd ride with him and could be ready to leave in five minutes. The sheriff told them to meet in front of the sheriff's office and jail. Holliman and his deputy returned to the office and grabbed two Winchester rifles and several boxes of cartridges.

Within five minutes the posse members had arrived, were sworn in and ready to ride. With the sheriff taking the lead they headed out of town in the direction the Heller gang had gone. The trail was easy enough to follow until the gang split up.

When they reached the point where the gang had split up Sheriff Holliman held up his hand and the posse stopped.

"They've split up right here, but you can be sure both trails will end up in the Sierras. You can also bet they'll circle around and meet up somewhere around Havilah. They could be setting us up for an ambush by splitting the posse up. We won't go along with their scheme.

"Instead of splittin' up we'll stay together and follow the tracks of the three riders. It's my guess that Garth, Max and Dooley Heller make up the threesome," Sheriff Holliman stated.

"The last time a posse was on their trail they lost 'em about five miles out of town. Sherman, you know the area around Havilah better than anyone around these parts, what is your take on where they could be losing a posse?" posse member Bill Hostetter asked.

"If'n I was gonna lose a posse, I'd use Dinky Creek near the old Hutchinson place to do it. I'd cross the creek and head west for about a mile and then enter the creek and reverse my direction and ride upstream to where Sugar Loaf Creek comes into it.

"I'd go up Sugar Loaf about a mile and a half and take to the rocky terrain up there. There ain't a posse alive that could track them," Sherman stated.

"You're probably right, Sherman. One thing is for sure though. They'll eventually wind up somewhere in the High Sierras where I think their hideout is," Sheriff Holliman said.

The posse headed for the old Hutchinson place to see if Sherman was right. They found the Heller gang's tracks all right and they entered the creek just like Sherman had figured they'd do. But they never found the spot where they came out.

Finally the posse gave up and headed back into town. This wasn't going to look good to the townspeople, but you can't chase a ghost, and that's what the sheriff felt like they were doing. The sheriff's job very well could be on the line and he knew it better than anyone. But help was on the way traveling under an assumed name.

Chapter 8

Wichita, Kansas
November 2, 1879

Brian Sackett sat in the train depot office and answered questions about the shootings on the train. His recollection of what had happened jived exactly with that of Mike McManus. The man doing the questioning was the Wichita line supervisor who wanted to make a name for himself with upper management.

"Did you not take into account the safety of the passengers while involved in the shootout?" Dexter Thorndike asked in a harsh tone of voice.

"I think both Mike and I did, that's why we engaged the men attempting to holdup the train," Brian said.

"What if some innocent bystander had been killed; would your heroics have been worth it then?" Thorndike asked.

"What if we'd done nothing and a couple of them had been murdered by the train robbers? What would your questions be then? I'll tell you what your question would have been. *Why* didn't you do something to stop the robbers? That's what you would have wanted to know. You act like we're the guilty ones here," Brian snapped angrily.

"You just answer the questions, I'll provide the smart remarks," Thorndike replied.

"I haven't heard you say anything that could be mistaken for 'smart' since we walked in here. Mike and I went by the book from what he said and I'll take his judgment on that over yours any day," Brian shot back.

"You are very insolent, did you know that?" Thorndike said with a frown.

"And you're a pain in the...," Brian started to say, but saw McManus shake his head no.

"...neck," Brian finished getting a grin from McManus.

"I'm going to write this in my report, I hope you know that," the supervisor stated.

"Good. I just hope the higher ups have more brains than you do," Brian said and stood up to go.

"Where do you think you're going? I'm not through with you," Thorndike warned.

"Oh yeah, well, I'm through with you. You write what you want to in your report. As for me, I'm going to get something to eat. I'm starved, what about you, Mike?" Brian said as he walked to the office door.

"I'm right with you, Brian. Oh, and by the way, Thorndike, I go along with everything Sackett said," McManus said. Turning back to Brian, McManus said, "I know a good place to eat just down the street."

Thorndike was beside himself as he mumbled, "I'm sending a telegram off, post haste."

"Good we should be getting an answer very shortly then," McManus replied.

The two railroad detectives walked out of the office and once outside looked at one another and laughed.

"Can you believe that guy?" McManus asked.

"I can't, what about you?" Brian returned the question.

"He's a new one to me. He must have come from back east. Did you catch that accent?"

"Yeah, but don't ask me to tell you where it's from," Brian replied.

The two men went down the street to one of the nicer eateries in town that served a good lunch. They took a seat in the corner where they could watch the front door. Both men were in the habit of doing that as a precautionary measure. They didn't want their backs towards doors or windows.

They ordered a couple of beers and then walked up to a long counter where there was an area of cold cuts, cheese, bread, butter, and relishes. They made themselves a couple of large sandwiches and returned to their table.

They had just sat down and started enjoying their sandwich when a woman peered into the café through the front door. When she saw the two of them seated against the far wall, she entered the saloon somewhat timidly.

Both men watched as the woman walked hurriedly in their direction while casting looks at the gawking patrons. She certainly wasn't a saloon girl. She looked as though she had good breeding.

She walked up in front of the two detectives and stood very erect as she asked, "Are you the railroad detectives that were involved in a shootout on a train recently?"

The two men looked at one another and then returned their gaze toward the woman. Mike McManus nodded his head and said, "Yes, ma'am we are. My name is Mike McManus and this is my partner, Brian Sackett."

"I'd like to talk to you both. May I sit down?" she said looking around at the still staring male patrons.

"Yes, have a seat," Brian said as he and McManus stood up.

The woman pulled a chair out from the table and sat down. Brian smiled as he and McManus once again took their seats.

"What is it you want to talk to us about?" McManus asked.

"My name is Heidi Lawless and I am taking my deceased husband's body down to Texas where we moved from, and I was wondering how safe his casket will be on the train," she said.

McManus smiled slightly as he said, "It'll be safer than everyone else on the train."

His comment brought a slight grin to Sackett's face, but the woman remained very serious. She looked from one man to the other and then stated.

"I mean...will anyone try and open the casket?" she asked.

"Not if it's sealed properly," McManus said.

"I know you're probably wondering why I'm concerned about something like that, but it's for the safety of the other passengers. You see my husband died of a case of cholera and I wouldn't want anyone else to come down with it," she said, getting the attention of the two men.

"Oh, I see. You can be sure that no one will open that casket. We'll put a warning label on it stating it is not to be tampered with due to an infectious disease," McManus said dropping the smile.

"Oh, that's a load off my mind," the woman said with a sigh and started to get up from her chair.

"Would you care for some lunch?" Sackett asked.

"No, thank you. I ate at the hotel where I'm staying. So how will I go about getting the warning sign put on the casket so it's official looking?" she asked.

"Where is the casket now?" McManus asked.

"It's at the train station. The station master said he would keep an eye on it."

"We'll go down there as soon as we finish our lunch and post the sign. When does your train leave?" McManus asked.

"Not until tomorrow morning. I'll rest easy knowing that my husband's remains will not be tampered with," she said with a smile.

With those final words she turned and walked out of the saloon. The two men watched her walk away, along with every other man in the place. Once she had exited the saloon McManus spoke.

"I hate hauling dead bodies of people who died because of some contagious disease. It makes the passengers a little uneasy should they find out."

"I can see why. Have you heard of any cases of cholera in the area?" Brian asked.

"No, but then I haven't been here for awhile. I've been down in Texas, remember," McManus said.

"I don't know about you, Mike, but that whole thing seems suspicious to me," Brian said.

"Let's take a walk down to the newspaper office. If they don't know anything we'll check with a doctor here in town," McManus said.

"Lead the way, Mike; I'm right with you," Brian said.

Brian and McManus started for the newspaper office, but when they saw a doctor's shingle decided to check with him first. The doctor told them that the Lawless couple had indeed visited a place in the midst of a cholera outbreak. His statement calmed the detectives' concerns.

The next day, November 3rd, Brian and McManus boarded the train that was carrying the body of the deceased Mr. Lawless. His wife, Heidi Lawless insisted on riding in the baggage car with her husband's casket. Usually this wasn't allowed, but she had managed to obtain a release from Dexter Thorndike the line superintendent, giving her the authority to do so.

The casket had a warning label on it that the casket contained the body of a man who'd died from cholera.

Mrs. Lawless seemed somewhat nervous, but McManus said it was probably due to losing her husband and perhaps this was the first time she'd ever ridden on a train. Brian wasn't sure, but something didn't seem right about the whole thing.

As the train pulled out with the two detectives riding in the last car, Brian glanced at two men seated a few rows up ahead. It was the difference in size of the two men that caught Brian's attention. The man seated next to the aisle towered over the other man. Then Brian noticed how the man towered over everyone on the train; even him.

The first name that came to Brian's mind was Cable Dutton. The mere thought of Dutton sent a chill down Brian's spine. When a man like Dutton threatens to kill you, you'd better take the threat seriously. Brian had to find out if the man was Dutton or not.

"Mike I'll be right back. I want to check those two men out who are seated up ahead of us," Brian said and was up before McManus could stop him.

Brian walked up to the front of the car and pretended to be looking for something outside. As he turned around he made it a point to give the tall man seated next to the aisle a good look see.

Brian instantly recognized the big man although Dutton quickly turned his face away. Sensing that Brian had recognized him, however, Dutton drew his gun and fired two shots at Brian. At that very moment, however, the train's engineer set the brakes hard because of a herd of buffalo crossing the tracks ahead.

The sudden stop caused everyone to lurch forward, thus when Dutton fired the first shot at Sackett, he hit the man seated in front of him. Dutton's second shot went wild due to the violent

65

jerking of the train. Brian stumbled backwards, but drew his gun as he regained his balance.

Brian fired one shot that took Dutton's right ear off. Dutton let out a painful yowl and quickly put his hand to the side of his head. Brian quickly fired a second shot that hit the big man in the head.

Dutton fell backwards and fell in to the aisle. He twitched violently for several seconds and then died. The man with Dutton took up the fight at this point and put two slugs into Brian.

Brian fell in the aisle between the seats and just lay there. As the man got up to run out of the car, Mike McManus pulled his gun, but couldn't get a shot off due to the people in the car being in the way. When the man reached the car door McManus had a wide open shot at him and fired off two rounds that sent the man sprawling against the door. He died on the spot as had Dutton.

Some passengers were scurrying for cover, while some of the men pulled their guns ready to open fire on whoever they deemed was in the wrong. Fortunately they didn't actually start firing at anyone.

One of the passengers was a doctor and he immediately checked Brian's wounds. Brian had been fortunate again; his wounds were flesh wounds and not life threatening. One of the wounds, however, was more severe than the other one.

Brian's wound was to his right arm and the bullet had damaged a tendon so badly that Brian would have trouble drawing and firing a pistol with his right hand. He'd have to learn to shoot with his left hand.

Due to the fact that Brian was right handed it looked as though his work as a railroad detective was at an end. It had been short lived, but at least he was alive. It looked like his future would be back on the Sackett ranch. In a way Brian was thankful for the incident that would send him home. He had missed his family.

Raymond D. Mason

Chapter 9

Bakersfield, California
November 12, 1879

Brent rode into the town of Bakersfield at high noon sporting a two week growth of beard. He felt more at ease since he had crossed over the Tehachapi Mountain Range, feeling he had left his troubles far behind him.

The first place he headed was a saloon where he downed a couple of cold beers and then he found a bath house. It felt good to get a week's worth of dust off his body. His next stop was a café and a hot meal.

He learned that Bakersfield had a population of almost eight hundred people. The town sheriff was a new man replacing the old town marshal they had employed earlier, but because of his age and the fact he had to use a cane to get around, the town disincorporated itself so the marshal quit since he had no one to pay his salary.

Brent suddenly had an idea. Why not see about hiring on as a deputy. He'd use an assumed name naturally and since he was new to California he could use just about any name he chose to use. That move would give him some cover as he set out to blend in with the locals and establish himself as a law abiding citizen.

Brent went to the general store and got some new clothes. He also bought himself a new hat and new boots. He kept his old pair of boots, however, and wore them from time to time until he got the new ones broken in. The last touch to his new look was a shave and a haircut. Looking in the mirror, if he hadn't known who he was he wouldn't have recognized himself.

Once Brent was decked out and more presentable he went to speak with the sheriff. Brent felt like a dandy when he entered the sheriff's office. The sheriff, however, treated him with more respect than Brent would have thought possible.

"Hello, Sheriff," Brent said with a smile, "I heard that you're a new hire as sheriff here in Bakersfield, is that right?"

"Yes, that's right. What can I do for you, Sir?" the sheriff asked.

"I was wondering if you might need an experienced lawman as one of your deputies," Brent asked, coming straight to the point.

"You sayin' you have experience at wearing a badge?" Sheriff Holliman said.

"Yes...oh, don't let the clothing fool you, but this is what they wanted us to wear when I *'deputied'* with Bat Masterson back in Dodge City," Brent said, bending the truth to a point that it was unrecognizable.

Holliman's ears perked up when he heard the name Bat Masterson.

"You mean you worked the streets with Bat Masterson?"

"I did. Not for long, mind you. I moved on to Santa Fe and Silver City," Brent went on.

"Well, I don't know that we're as exciting a town as those places, but we did just have ourselves a bank robbery not long ago," the sheriff said eagerly.

"Really, a bank robbery, eh," Brent said with a head nod. "Did you catch the men responsible?"

"Well...no we lost their trail about five miles out of town. We're pretty sure who they were though," the sheriff stated.

"Oh, and who might that be?"

"The Heller gang," the sheriff said proudly.

"That wouldn't be the Bart Heller gang...; no it couldn't be them. Wyatt and the boys got them last year up in the Dakota badlands," Brent said running a bluff.

"Do you mean Wyatt Earp?" Holliman asked wide eyed.

"Yeah, Wyatt and Morgan shot it out with Bart and his gang and cut all three of 'em down," Brent said seriously. "I'm sure you read about it."

"Oh, yeah...in the paper," Holliman replied and then said as an afterthought. "But, I might be hiring myself right out of a job if I hire you."

Brent chuckled, "No that's not likely. I'm on my way up north and thought I'd check to see if you needed a deputy. You see...I got into a crooked poker game and I'm now looking for work, if you get my drift."

"Oh, well that's different. I guess I could hire you and have you looking into the bank holdup. Maybe you could turn up something that would help me get elected come election time," Holliman said thoughtfully.

"That's a possibility," Brent said.

"Let me talk to the city council and see what they say. If they say okay, you're hired. Oh, I guess I should know your name, huh," the sheriff said with a grin.

"Yes, it's Bart Hardin," Brent said evenly.

"Not any kin to Wes Hardin are you?" the sheriff asked.

"A cousin on my father's side," Brent said and then added, "But we don't want people to know it, what with his reputation and all."

"I can see why," the sheriff grinned.

"I'll check back tomorrow and see if you have any news from the council. Say, around ten in the morning? Until then if you should need me I'll be in the hotel down the street," Brian said.

"That's fine, yes that'll do just fine," Holliman said.

Brent and the sheriff shook hands and Brent headed down the street to the hotel. After going to his room he lay on the bed and thought about his next move. A smile slowly spread across his face as he lay there staring up at the ceiling, deep in thought.

If this worked out all right he could be home free. No one would think of looking for him here in Bakersfield and wearing a badge to boot. In fact, he may carry this deputy thing even further; like all the way to the Sacramento area.

Brent dozed off and slept for about four hours. When he awoke it was dark out and he was starving. He got up, washed his face and headed down the street to the nearest place where he could get a meal. It was a small café that stayed open until nine o'clock in the evening. All the sign said over the front of the place was 'Café'.

The waitress took his order and he sat back and observed what few patrons there were in the place. When the waitress returned to his table with his order he asked her if she was the owner or just worked there.

"I'm the owner who works here," the woman said with a grin.

"Is your husband the cook?" Brent asked.

"Yes, as a matter of fact he is. And, I might add, he's a very jealous man where I'm concerned and he's mighty handy with a carving knife," she said evenly.

"Hey, I wasn't getting overly familiar with you, ma'am, I was just wondering. There's a good chance I'll be going to work here in town and I simply wanted to know a little about the people who own the café where I'll be taking most of my meals. So, you can tell your husband he can put away his carving knife because I'm not the least bit interested in you personally," Brent said taking on a hard tone.

The woman smiled slightly and said, "That's good, because now I can tell you the truth. No, I'm not married and the cook is fifty eight years old and not related to me."

Brent couldn't hold back the smile that bubbled over into a chuckle and then a hearty laugh. The woman smiled to see he had taken it all good naturedly.

"I always say that to strangers in town and since I've never seen you before wanted to make sure you didn't get any funny ideas," the woman said and then added, "Let me get you some more coffee, Mr. ...?"

"Hardin...Bret Hardin," Brent said forgetting that he'd told the sheriff his first name was Bart.

"It's nice to meet you Mr. Hardin. My name is Linda Thomas. Is there something else I could do for you?"

"I'm sure there is, but I'll keep it to myself for now," Brent said off handedly.

Linda looked at him hard for a few seconds and then said, "I think that would be a wise thing to do."

Brent cocked his head to one side and said, "I think you're applying the wrong meaning to what I just said. I wasn't being off color."

Linda's face reddened slightly and she quickly excused herself and went back into the kitchen. She caught a peek at Brent through the cook's service window.

Brent enjoyed the meal and after having a last cup of coffee paid his check, leaving a healthy tip. When he got to the door he looked back and asked, "What time do you open for breakfast?"

"Five," Linda called back.

"I'll see you at six," Brent said and walked out.

Brent walked down the street four doors to the Buckboard Saloon. There were only about a dozen customers in the place, but there was a card game going on. Brent made his way to the table where four men were playing Five Card Stud poker.

Brent watched for a couple of hands and determined that they were all locals and none of them appeared to be a card sharps. After he determined the game was on the up and up he asked if he could sit in on it.

"Well, I suppose so. We don't know you though," one of the men said.

"I don't know you men either," Brent said with a smile. "But you may come to know me quite well. There's a good chance I'll be a deputy sheriff here in Bakersfield. The name is Bret Hardin," Brent said.

"In that case, sit down Bret and take a load off. My handle is Archie Farmer, but I'm a rancher."

"Nice to make your acquaintance, Archie," Brent replied with a chuckle.

"These three are Neil, Denver and Bud. They don't have a last name because their folks had bad memories," Archie joked.

"Gentlemen," Brent said with a smile as he took a seat and then asked, "What's the limit?"

"Table stakes and you can only raise a bet twice. As you probably noticed we're playing Five Card Stud, and there're no game changes," Archie said.

"Sounds good to me," Brent said with a grin.

By the end of the game Brent had won over a hundred and fifty dollars and made friends of the four men in the game. After buying them all a drink he went back to his hotel room and straight to bed.

The next day he had breakfast at the same café where he'd had supper. The woman seemed happy to see him and suggested he sit at the small counter where they'd be able to talk between orders.

Linda was a beautiful woman with a quick wit and a warm personality. Brent liked her sassiness because it reminded him of Julia, the love of his life. Linda was attracted to the tall, good looking man she knew as Bret Hardin.

After breakfast Brent made the short walk to the sheriff's office where he met several members of the city council. The sheriff had just finished laying out his reasoning for wanting them to hire a deputy sheriff to spell him at times. After they met 'Bret Harding' they were in full agreement to hiring him.

The sheriff looked curiously at Brent and said, "You introduced yourself as Bret Hardin, but yesterday I thought you told me it was Bart Hardin?"

"No, Sheriff, I said Bret; you must have misunderstood me. But, hey…if you want to call me Bart you go right ahead. Like the man said, 'I don't care what you call me, just don't call me late to supper'," Brent said getting a laugh from all those present.

Brent knew he would have to be careful with the name changes. Hopefully he wouldn't run into someone that knew him as one of his other aliases, and especially not as Brent Sackett.

Chapter 10

"I guess you can start today if you want to, Bret," the sheriff said once the council had given their okay.

"That's fine with me, Sheriff. I'd like for you to give me as much rundown on this Heller gang as you can, because they will be my first point of business. I want to get them before they have a chance to spend all the money they stole from the bank robbery here last week," Brent said.

"You know about that do you?" the sheriff said.

"Yes, you told me about it yesterday and last night I played cards with some of the town folks and they gave me a little more insight," Brent replied.

"Yes, yes. Well, we were able to follow them so far and then we lost their trail. If you want to see if you can pick it up again I'll send one of the men who rode in the posse that day and he can show you where," the sheriff stated.

"That's fine. I'd like to get right on that, if you don't mind, Sheriff," Brent said.

"Okay, let me get hold of old Sherman Trotter and he'll show you the spot. He was a scout for the cavalry in his younger days. He could smell an Indian two miles away. Now he smells a whiskey bottle two miles away. A free drink he smells even further away than that," the sheriff said.

Suddenly a man burst into the sheriff's office known only by the name of Alabama and said in a rush, "Come quick, Sheriff. There's trouble down at the freight office."

"What is it, Alabama?" the sheriff asked.

"I saw two men holding it up when I came by. They had the drop on the freight driver," Alabama said.

"Come on Bret let's go see what this is all about."

"I'm right with you, Sheriff," Brent said and then asked Alabama, "That's strange that they'd be robbing a freight wagon in town and in broad daylight."

'I only know what these old eyes of mine told me they saw," Alabama stated.

The three men hurried to the freight office and when they got to the corner of the building stopped so they could observe what was taking place without being seen.

There were two men holding their guns on the freight driver. The sheriff looked at Brent and asked, "How would you handle this?"

"You stay here and watch me. When I give you the high sign, come a runnin'. No one knows me around town yet; not as a deputy sheriff, anyway, so maybe I can get the drop on them," Brent said getting a 'thumbs up' from the sheriff.

Brent made sure his deputy sheriff's badge was concealed as he casually strolled around the corner and in the direction of the freight office. The office set back towards the rear of the building next to it, thus giving the freight wagons more space for loading and unloading and turning around.

"Howdy," Brent said as he casually strolled up to the two men holding guns on the other two men.

"What do you want, mister," one of the gunmen said with a frown.

"I'm looking for the freighter. I have a load of freight I'd like to send up to Sacramento," Brent said.

"We're busy right now as I'm sure you can see," one of the men said. "You see, I'm going to kill this no good for having his way with my wife."

"Why are you angry at him? Shouldn't it be your woman you're mad at? She's the one who was untrue to you, not this man," Brent said in a casual tone of voice.

"I'll take care of her in my own way, but this no good is going to die right here and now," the man replied.

"Let's see if I get this straight. You were played for a sucker by your wife and now you're going to be a sucker again and go to prison for murder? Is that right? That is if they don't hang you. Now what I'd do is...," Brent said, but was cut off.

"I don't care what you would do. I'm going to kill this no good sob," the man repeated himself.

"What if I told you that this man isn't the only man in town who has been having his way with your wife? What would you do then?" Brent asked.

The man looked at him with a questioning look and said, "Who else has been seeing her?"

"Let's see...the city council, the sheriff, the bartender, the doctor, the lawyer, the banker, the baker, and...oh yeah, we can't forget about an Indian Chief," Brent said and then in a lightning draw pulled his gun and smashed it across the man's gun hand thus knocking his gun to the ground.

When the man instinctively bent down to retrieve his gun Brent hit him across the head with the barrel of his gun, knocking the man out cold.

The second man instantly dropped his gun and raised his hands high over his head, "I wasn't going to hurt anyone," man said quickly.

"You were holding your gun on them. If he'd shot this man you would have been an accomplice to the whole thing," Brent said.

By this time the sheriff and Alabama were running towards Brent and the others.

"Nice work, Bret; you got him," the sheriff said with a wide smile, obviously feeling good about the work of his new hire.

"Do you know this guy, Sheriff?" Brent asked.

"Everybody in town knows Rufus Hubble...or should I say half the town knows Rufus and the other half knows his wife Mavis, if you get my drift," the sheriff said.

"I kind of gathered that by our little conversation. I hope I didn't hit him too hard," Brent said looking down at the man who hadn't moved since being pistol whipped.

"Alabama go over to the watering trough and get a hat full of water and see if we can wake Rufus up," the sheriff ordered.

Alabama started to go but stopped and picked up Rufus's hat to use as a container. He filled it at the trough and hurried back to where the others were standing.

"Splash him," the sheriff said.

Alabama threw the water towards Rufus's face but missed and threw it on the sheriff's boots. Alabama looked at the sheriff with a sheepish look on his face as the sheriff stood staring down at his wet boots.

The sheriff raised his eyes towards Alabama and asked, "What kind of a shot is that? The water was meant for Rufus's face, not my boots."

"I'm sorry, Sheriff, my hand slipped off the hat brim," Alabama replied.

"What was it you said you were during the War Between the States?" the sheriff asked.

Alabama stood there with a half grin on his face and said, "I was a sniper."

The sheriff looked at Brent and then back at Alabama and said, "How many of your own men did you shoot?"

"None...that I know of," Alabama said.

Just then Mavis Hubbell rounded the corner and started towards the sheriff. When she saw her husband lying on the ground she stopped in her tracks and asked, "Is he dead, Sheriff?"

"No, Mavis he's not dead, but your lover boy over there almost bit it. Rufus was going to kill him until my new deputy stopped him," the sheriff said.

"My lover boy, did you say?" Mavis responded. "Sheriff, you know how jealous Rufus is of me. He ordered a new plow last month and Clete delivered it this morning and met Rufus as he was driving back into town. He came home and accused me of having a dalliance with Clete. We had a big row and he left in a huff with our hired hand threatening to kill Clete," Mavis said in a rush.

They turned and looked at Rufus just as Alabama returned with another hat full of water and threw it in Rufus's face this time. Rufus immediately snapped to consciousness and tried to get up. He was in too much pain to even notice Mavis standing there with the sheriff and his new deputy.

Ever so gently Rufus put his hand on the goose egg Brent had raised on his head. He checked his fingertips to see if there was any blood and when he saw there wasn't, he breathed a sigh of relief. It was only then that he saw his wife standing beside the sheriff.

"She caused this whole thing, Sheriff. She's been seeing that Clete Hammons and I caught 'em today," Rufus said as he slowly and shakily got to his feet.

"Just what did you see, Rufus?" the sheriff asked.

"He was on the road after having been out to see her, that's what I saw. I don't have to have a building fall on me to know what's going on," Rufus stated.

Brent listened to Rufus's statement and then pointed towards Clete and said, "Now let's hear what this man has to say about it."

Clete stood slightly behind Brent and said, "I have just one question to ask Rufus."

"What is it you dirty lowdown skunk?" Rufus said with a sneer.

"Did you check the barn when you got home?" Clete asked.

"Why would I want to check the barn?" Rufus asked with a confused look on his face.

"If you had you would have seen that new plow you ordered awhile back. I delivered it today and I had Sid with me to help me get it off my wagon if you'll think about it. We were there all of fifteen minutes," Clete snapped.

Rufus looked bewildered for a moment before saying, "Oh."

"That's all you've got to say? How about apologizing to me for threatening my life and for accusing me of something I didn't do," Clete stated.

"Yeah," Rufus said sheepishly.

"Yeah, what," Clete replied.

"Yeah, I could do that," Rufus added.

"Oh, never mind. You're too stupid to understand what I'm getting at," Clete said and started to walk away.

"Do you want to press charges against Rufus, Clete?" the sheriff called after him.

"No, no...he's the one with knot on his head so let's just leave it at that. But if he ever comes after me with a gun again...I'll shoot him as dead as I would a rabid dog," Clete said looking back at the small gathering.

Raymond D. Mason

Chapter 11

Sackett Ranch
November 26, 1879

The first snow of the wintry season had just started to fall when Brian Sackett rode up to the family's ranch house. Although the hour was quite late there were still several lamps burning in the downstairs rooms. Brian trudged up the steps of the large front porch and stopped before knocking on the door.

Back when he had left the ranch he left in a surly, moody state of mind. He hoped the family would accept him back into the fold, so to speak. Finally he rapped on the door and stood waiting for someone to answer.

AJ Sackett opened the door and before he saw who was standing there said, "What are you doing out on a night like this?"

When AJ recognized Brian he broke into a huge smile and threw his arms around his brother in a bear hug. The two brothers patted each other on the back as they expressed their joy in seeing one another.

"Welcome home, little brother," AJ said with a wide grin.

"It's good to be home, AJ. Of course, as you can see I won't be much good to you in a gunfight," Brian said extending his wounded hand out so AJ could see it.

"Hey, you never were anyway, so what's new," AJ said feigning seriousness, but then broke into a laugh.

Brian laughed and shook his head at his brother's wise crack. The two had always tried to get one up on the other one and it looks like AJ was picking up where they had left off.

"Well, come on inside where it's warm," AJ said and then noticed Brian's horse. "Let's put your horse in the barn first, though."

The two brothers walked out to the hitching rail and talked about what had been happening around the ranch as they led the horse to the barn. Brian sensed that all was not well on the Sackett ranch.

"What's eatin' at you, AJ? You've done a lot of talking about a problem, but you haven't said what the problem is. Is it Pa's health? Is something going on here I should be made aware of before I see the rest of the family? What?" Brian questioned.

"Hoof and mouth disease, Brian" AJ said seriously. "We're afraid the cattle are infected."

Brian looked stunned at the news. He'd heard there had been a few cases in the area from a man he'd met on the train. If their cattle were infected it could cost them their entire herd.

"When did you discover this?" Brian asked as they reached the barn and opened the door.

"Two days ago. We're not sure that's what it is, but we'll know shortly. We've got an inspector coming out to check them out. If it is hoof and mouth, we could lose everything. You know how the market is right now; a setback like this could bankrupt us," AJ stated.

"How's the rest of the family taking it?" Brian asked as the two of them led the horse to a stall.

"You know them; they all have that Sackett resolve that we'll overcome it. I wish Brent was here. We might need all the help we can muster to get through this," AJ said honestly.

"Yeah, but the chances of that are slim and none. When's the last time you heard from him?"

"It's been awhile. He should be in California by now if everything went all right. I just hope no one recognizes him out there and he winds up in jail," AJ said as Brian pulled the saddle from his horse.

The continued to talk about things happening there on the ranch while Brian curried the horse down and tossed a pitchfork full of hay into a manger.

Once they had cared for the horse they went back to the main house. The rest of the family was in bed already and Brian didn't want to wake them. He and AJ talked in the large kitchen over a cup of coffee and Brian filled him in on what he'd been up to.

AJ looked at the wounded hand of Brian's and shook his head as he commented, "That bullet sure did its work on that hand."

"I've been practicing a left handed draw and I'm getting pretty good at it. I can fire a pistol all right with my left hand, but I'm having some trouble firing a rifle," Brian said and paused before asking.

"Not to change the subject, but...have you seen Terrin lately?" Brian asked about the woman who was the reason he'd left the ranch.

"Yeah, I see her quite often. I don't know if you know it or not, but she moved to Abilene," AJ said taking on a serious expression.

"She did? When did this happen?" Brian asked quickly.

"She got a job working in the bank there and moved her belongings into Mrs. Stillman's Boarding House not long after you left to work for the railroad," AJ said evenly and then asked. "Do you still have feelings for her?"

Brian thought for a moment and said, "Yes, I guess I do. I was so hurt when I found out about the guy she had gotten involved with that I just wanted to be as far from her as possible. But...I guess I still have feelings for her."

AJ nodded his head slowly and took a deep breath as he said, "I was afraid of that."

Brian looked quickly at his brother with a slight questioning frown and asked, "Why?"

AJ took another deep breath and said, "I've been seeing her on a friendly basis, you know. But, the truth is Brian...I've started having some very strong feelings for her."

Brian held a steady gaze on his brother for several torturous seconds and then grinned as he said, "AJ, you know I'd be the first to congratulate you if you were to tie the knot, be it with Terrin or someone else. She's a wonderful woman and you'd make a great couple," Brian said.

Another large exhale by AJ showed his relief in having to break the news to Brian about his feelings for Terrin Gibbons.

Brian and AJ had met Terrin quite by accident when they were all three held captive by a gang of Comancheros. They had managed to escape from the gang and Brian had fallen in love with the beautiful woman.

Terrin had also fallen for Brian, but was swept off her feet by a banker who turned out to be in cahoots with a gang of outlaws. He had been killed while involved in a scheme to rob his own bank which had brought the liaison between her and Brian to an abrupt end.

AJ recalled how Brian had moped around the house for some time after he and Terrin had parted ways.

Terrin had loved both Brian and the banker she had worked with, but lost both men. After Terrin had taken a job at the bank in Abilene, AJ had been a sympathetic ear for Terrin and he too had fallen in love with her. He had worried about Brian's reaction to the news, but now felt relieved that his brother seemed to be over her.

It had been the break up of their romance that had caused Brian to go to work for the railroad. He just wanted to get as far away as he could and get his thoughts together. Now he'd have to change his plans, but wouldn't let on about his feelings for AJ's sake.

Having cared for Brian's horse they returned to the house and said goodnight. Brian went up to his bedroom and prepared for bed. It was good to be home again, even if AJ's news about his feelings for Terrin had come unexpectedly. He certainly couldn't blame AJ seeing as how he had sworn he was through with Terrin before leaving.

Brian looked into the mirror and stared at his face for several seconds. He thought about the things he had said to AJ when he had broken up with Terrin and slowly shook his head.

"Someday, Brian Sackett, you may learn to keep your mouth shut where women are concerned."

Chapter 12

**Bakersfield, Calif.
November 26, 1879**

Brent Sackett opened the post office door to allow a lady to pass through first. She smiled at him and said, "Why, thank you, Mr. Hardin."

Brent smiled and asked, "Have we met?"

"No, but everyone in town knows about our new deputy sheriff and how you handled that dangerous situation at the freight office the other day," the woman said.

"Oh that, it was nothing really," Brent said. "Just a little matter of a misunderstanding; you know how those things can be."

"Well, we all feel a lot safer knowing we have a lawman like you in town now," the woman replied.

It turned out the woman Brent was speaking to wasn't a customer, but one of the post office employees. She went behind the counter and then turned and looked back at Brent.

"I suppose you came in for the sheriff's mail."

"Yes, Ma'am, the sheriff said he was expecting some things and asked me to fetch them for him," Brent answered.

The woman went to a bin and picked up a bundle of various types of paperwork and wanted posters. She returned to where Brent was waiting and handed them to him. He glanced down at the bundle of wanted posters and did a double take. The top poster had his picture on it and a $2,000 reward.

Brent quickly covered the poster bearing his likeness and told the woman behind the counter goodbye. He went outside and around the corner of the building where no one could see him. There, he removed the four wanted posters with his photo on them and ripped them up.

The last thing Brent needed now was for his picture to be posted all over town and possibly the entire state of California. He figured, however, that other lawmen in the area would be receiving the same posters. He'd have to be ready to leave town in a hurry should other lawmen come poking around. It would be just his luck that one of them would remember the wanted poster on him.

Seeing as how it was nearing noon, Brent dropped the rest of the mail off at the sheriff's office and went down the street to the 'Café'. He found a table and ordered the lunch special and then sat back and watched people going about their business on the street out front.

Brent's meal had just been served when two men on horseback entered town from the south. Brent eyed them for a moment and suddenly caught sight of a badge pinned on one of the men's jacket.

"Just what I need more lawmen," Brent said as he watched the men closely.

They rode directly to the sheriff's office and stopped. Brent watched them as they both sat astraddle their mounts for a moment before stepping down. The older of the two turned and stared directly at the café, but was unable to see through the window due to the sun's glare.

Brent knew he couldn't take a chance on being identified again, and figured on leaving Bakersfield, continuing his trip north to Sacramento. This would be as good a time as any to say adios to Bakersfield.

Brent called the café owner and asked if he could have his food wrapped. It was only natural that the owner figured it had to do with legal business and hurriedly prepared him a bag lunch.

Keeping a low profile Brent headed down the street to the livery stable where he'd left his horse. He saddled it and told the stableman that he was going to check on a tip about the Heller gang. That would keep the sheriff satisfied for several hours as well as keep the two lawmen at bay.

The spirited palomino was ready to hit the trail again. Brent gave it, its head and let it set a fast pace out of town. After a couple of miles he reined the horse to an easy gallop allowing it to catch its wind.

As Brent rode along he considered life on the run. This was what the rest of his life would be if he couldn't shake his past. Always looking over his shoulder, afraid that every lawman he saw was out looking for him. He wanted to rest, but it looked like there would be none for awhile.

Brent had left town without anymore supplies than those he always kept in his bedroll and saddlebags. He wasn't sure of how far it was to the next town, but hoped it wasn't too far. If he could find a general store somewhere he'd stock up on supplies and head for the mountains where he'd be less likely to run into lawmen.

Brent headed for the town of Glennville which was thirty miles northeast of Bakersfield. The town was at an elevation of around 3,000 feet on mountainous terrain. The farther Brent got from Bakersfield the better he felt.

He didn't arrive in the small town until around 9 pm that night. There was one saloon that was open so that's where Brent stopped. He went in and ordered what little they offered in the way of food and downed a couple of cool beers.

Brent was just about to order his third beer when three men pushed the saloon doors open and stopped in the doorway to survey the entire room before entering. Brent knew they were either troublemakers or men on the dodge. He was right on both counts.

The taller of the three men's gaze stopped when it landed on Brent. Brent gave him a hard look which caused the man to say something to the other two. They also gave Brent a hard stare. It was only then that Brent realized he was still wearing his deputy sheriff's badge.

Brent couldn't hold back a grin when he realized what had caused the three men's reactions.

He chuckled and broke off his stare down with the three. As soon as he looked away the three of them got their heads together real quick like.

When Brent got up to go to the bar and order another beer he walked up next to the three. He looked at the taller man and nodded slightly. The man returned the nod and then turned to face Brent.

"I notice you're wearing a deputy sheriff's badge; are you the law here in Glennville now?" the man asked.

"Me, no; actually I took this off the deputy down in Bakersfield on my way out of town," Brent said and chuckled.

"Is that right? And just who might you be to your friends?" the man asked.

"Now why would you ask my name in that way? We're not friends," Brent replied.

"No, but I'll be friends with any man who takes a badge off a marshal, sheriff, or a deputy sheriff," the man said and grinned.

"Oh, I see. Well in that case...friend...my name is Ben Dalton. And who might you be when you're at home?" Brent asked.

"I'm Garth Heller and these are my brothers, Max and Dooley. You might have heard of us?" Garth asked.

"No, actually I haven't. I just arrived in California awhile back. I'm headed north so I don't know anyone around here," Brent stated.

"Where're you from, Ben?" Garth asked.

"Here and there, you name it and I've probably been there."

"I hear a Texas drawl. What part of Texas are you from?" Garth asked.

Brent stiffened and a frown came to his face as he said, "You're an awful nosey type, Garth. There're some things a man doesn't want to talk about and that's one I don't want to discuss; not with you and not with anyone," Brent said sharply.

"Hey, don't get your dander up, I was just asking. I like to know a lot about someone I'm considering asking to ride with us," Garth answered.

"Oh, and is that what you were about to do? Ask me to ride with you boys? And why might I be interested in doing that?" Brent said evenly.

"You look like a man who could use some money, that's all. Like I said, if you were from around here you'd have heard of the Heller gang. We run from Sacramento to Bakersfield and parts west. We're in need of a new man and I think you might be that man," Garth said seriously.

"I'm headed for Sacramento and I don't have time to kill knocking off banks in one horse towns, if you get my drift," Brent said.

"How does one bank job with over two hundred thousand dollars in it sound to you?"

Brent pursed his lips and said, "Keep talking."

"There's a bank in Fresno that is brimming over with cattle money. We're heading up that way tomorrow morning to knock it over. Like I said, we need another man. I take it you're good with a gun?" Garth said.

"If you'd like a demonstration I'm open to it," Brent said confidently.

"How do you mean that?"

"Let's take one bullet out of our gun and then have a draw off. The one whose hammer falls on the empty chamber first is the winner," Brent said.

"I'm game," Garth said and started to take a bullet from his cylinder.

"No, no...I'll take the bullet from your gun and you take it from mine. That way we'll be sure no one messes up. If one of us does, it means his life," Brent said with a grin.

"You're a shrewd man, Ben Dalton, I like that," Garth said.

The two men removed the bullet from each others pistol and then holstered their guns. Garth told Max to start counting and the two of them would draw down on the count of three.

Max started, "One...two...three," he said.

Brent had his gun drawn and the hammer snapped down on the empty chamber with Garth's gun just halfway out of its holster. His eyes were wide with the speed of the man he thought was named Ben Dalton.

"Man, you're fast, Ben. Why haven't I heard your name before?" Garth asked.

"Like I said, I move around a lot. California is where I hang my hat now," Brent said as he reloaded his pistol.

Raymond D. Mason

Chapter 13

Brent continued to drink with the Heller's until around midnight. Garth asked Brent where he was staying and was told he didn't have a place. Garth invited him to their hideout which was about two miles out of town.

The night was pitch black because there was no moon and the sky was overcast. This made it very difficult for Brent to know exactly where the hideout was located. He knew they had headed north and then cut off the main trail and took what appeared to be a deer path to a cabin that was at least two hundred yards off the trail.

There were two other men inside the cabin but they were asleep. Garth said he'd introduce Brent to them the following morning. Brent was in no hurry to meet them; he just wanted to get some shuteye, which he did as soon as his head hit a pillow.

The next morning Brent awoke to whispers of a couple of men talking near him. He lay there pretending to be asleep and took in all that was being said. He was the subject of their conversation.

"I don't like the idea that you're bringing some drifter in that we know nothing about, Garth. That's a sure way to get caught if you ask me," the unidentified man said.

"Look, Ned, we need another man if we're going to pull this job off. I think this guy is on the dodge and needs the money. The fact that he wouldn't even tell me where he is from confirms that as far as I'm concerned," Garth replied.

"He could be a plant by the law, though. You said yourself he was wearing a deputy sheriff's badge when you met him last night," Ned said.

"Look, I personally checked out Bakersfield before we hit the bank there and I know he wasn't the old sheriff's deputy. It was a guy a lot shorter than this man," Garth stated.

"Let me talk to him when he wakes up and I'll see if I can get some more information out of him. I just don't like the idea of a drifter being brought into the gang like this," Ned said firmly.

When the two stopped talking about him, Brent stretched and acted as though he had just awakened. He looked towards Garth Heller and sat up. He gave the man named Ned a quick look and took an immediate dislike to the man. Brent sat up and rubbed his eyes.

"Mornin'," Brent said without focusing on either man.

"How'd you sleep, Dalton?" Garth asked.

"Fine, but when you've been in the saddle as long as I've been you always sleep good," Brent replied.

Garth nodded and gave a glance towards Ned as he said, "I'd like to introduce you to Ned Hatcher. Ned, this is Ben Dalton."

"Dalton, huh," Ned replied. "I know some Dalton's up in the San Jose area. You wouldn't be related to them would you?"

"I could be; my old pappy was quite a rounder. There's no telling how many kinfolk I have scattered around the country," Brent answered.

"That's no answer," Ned snapped.

"It's the only one you're going to get, Slick," Brent replied with a hard look.

Ned started to get up out of his chair, but Garth put his hand on him and stopped him.

"Let's not get off on a bad start here. Ben, Ned here just wants to know a little more about you, that's all. Ned, I've seen Ben's draw and you ain't 'no' match for him, believe me," Garth stated.

"I'll tell you this and that's all you'll get from me. I'm from Texas originally. Does that satisfy you, Ned?" Brent said with a set jaw.

Ned held a steady gaze on Brent and finally nodded his head yes and said, "I'll accept that."

"You'll have to because that's all you're gettin'," Brent said and stood up. "So let me hear the details on this bank job in Fresno?" Brent said changing the subject and easing the tension that had built between Ned and him.

Garth laid out the plans for robbing the bank and when he finished Brent slowly shook his head negatively. Garth looked at him with a frown and asked, "What's the matter? You don't like the plan?"

101

"Nope, I don't. How have you boys survived as long as you have with plans like that for robbing a bank?" Brent stated.

"I suppose you have a better way, eh Dalton," Garth said with a bite to his words.

"I do. You want to go in like every other gang and rob a bank. Why not use your brains a little more than your guns," Brent said, looking at the two men.

Garth leaned back slightly and said, "Okay, I'll listen to what your suggestion is. Go ahead, Dalton, let's hear what you've got."

"Who is the least suspected person to be seen going into a bank; someone associated with the bank, right?"

The two men nodded slowly in agreement waiting for the point that Brent was going to make.

"And who is it the bankers fear the most?" Brent asked.

"Bank robbers," Ned said quickly.

"Huh uh...bank *auditors*. If you go about hitting the bank like you said, the whole town would be alerted to the possibility of a holdup from the time we ride in until the shootin' starts and there will be shooting believe me," Brent said.

"So what's your plan?" Garth asked.

"We send a telegram to the banker stating that an auditor from the government is coming to audit their books, but we only give him a few hours notice. We tell him we don't want to cause any undo problems for the customers so we will audit the books after banking hours. This will get the banker worrying more about his books than his money.

"I go in as the auditor and, Garth, you and Ned go in as customers, but hang around until all the other customers have left the bank. After I make like I've checked his books, I ask to see the safety features his bank has in place to protect against robbery. When he opens the vault we make our move," Brent said.

Ned frowned deeply as he said, "There's too much that could go wrong with a plan like that. I say we go in and take the money and shoot anyone who gets in our way."

"If there's as much money in that bank as Garth says it's going to be well guarded. Are you sure you want to get into a shootout with men who know how to handle guns and not just a bunch of storeowners?" Brent said firmly.

Garth nodded his head as he thought about what Brent had stated. He could see the merit in doing it that way and how the possibility of making a clean getaway was much better. The more he thought about it, the better Heller liked the idea.

"That sounds good to me. In fact, we could pull this job off with just three men. Of course, there'll be more involved than just three," Garth said.

"You can say that again," Brent replied. "In fact the other men will be busy creating a diversion. They'll be setting a few fires at each end of town. The more turmoil we can create in the streets of Fresno, the better our chances of making a clean getaway," Brent said.

Garth grinned and looked at Ned as he said, "What do you think of this drifter now, Ned? Pretty shrewd character, wouldn't you say," Heller said with a laugh.

Ned nodded his head in agreement. He too saw the worth in what Brent had just laid out. Why hadn't they thought of something like that before? Why did this drifter have to come up with a plan like this? The more he though about it the more he liked it and made his thoughts known.

"Dalton, I like the way you think," Ned said and looked at Garth. "I'm glad you brought this man in, Garth. It looks to me like you out did yourself," Ned grinned.

"Wake the others up and let's fill them in on how we're going to pull this off and what their role in this will be," Garth said as he started rousting the others out of their beds.

Chapter 14

Russell's Tank, Arizona

Clay Butler reined up at the only saloon he came to when he reached the small settlement of Flagstaff. He noticed several horses tied at the hitching rail, but didn't see the strawberry roan mare that the stableman in Flagstaff had said Bateman had bought from him.

Clay went into what served as a saloon in the small settlement and eyed the four men who were in the bar. They all four looked like hard cases who were just passing through, but weren't necessarily traveling together.

As Clay moved up to the bar to order a drink and give the rugged looking bartender a description of Bateman one of the four men moved in front of him. Butler stopped and gave the man a hard stare.

"Where are you from?" the man asked.

Clay looked towards the other three men to try and determine if they were partnered with this guy. Clay looked back at him and said, "Tucson...why?"

"I don't like your looks, that's why," the man said.

"Well, I can't help that, now can I," Butler said and started to go around the man.

"Hey, I ain't through with you," the man said and moved in front of Butler again.

"You may not be, but I'm through with you. Now get out of my way before one of us gets hurt bad, and it won't be me," Butler said with a deep frown.

The large, bearded man reached out to grab Clay by the shirt, but stopped short when he felt Clay's pistol shoved against his belly. The man's eyes widened as he glanced down at the Colt pressed against him. When Clay cocked the hammer back the man slowly moved off to one side with his hands held up shoulder high.

"Are we through here?" Clay asked.

"As long as you're holding that hog leg we are," the man said still holding a serious look on his face.

"Good," Clay said and moved up to the bar where he asked the man about Bateman, but never took his eyes off the four men in the room.

"I'm on the trail of a man traveling by himself. He's around five feet ten or eleven, weighs around a hundred eighty and has a narrow moustache. He dresses like a gambler; suit and a vest, black hat. Has he been by here?" Clay asked.

The barman nodded slowly and said, "Yeah, there was a man like stopped here about eight hours ago. He tried to get a card game up, but when he couldn't find anyone interested he had a drink and left. Do you want a drink?" the man asked.

"Yeah, I'll have a beer. Thanks for the information. Are these four regulars in here?" Butler asked.

"Nope, never saw them before. There ain't enough folks living around here for me to have too many regulars. I'd watch 'em if I was you," the bartender said under his breath. "They all look like they're trouble in the making."

"Yeah, I'd say so. What's the next settlement west of here?" Clay asked.

"I guess that would be the Kingman settlement," the barman said.

The four men continued to glare at Clay and he kept his eyes on them. After a minute or so two of the men got up and walked out. When they got to the door they gave another quick look back in Clay's direction before exiting.

The one Clay had the encounter with sat with the fourth man in the bar. The two of them talked in hushed voices and after a few minutes they too got up to leave. When they reached the door the man Clay had the run in with looked back and said, "I'll be seeing you down the trail, hoss."

"You'd better hope not," Clay replied and the man went on out to his horse.

Clay looked back at the bar man and asked, "You wouldn't happen to know which direction those two were heading, would you?"

"Yeah, I do. It just so happens that I heard them say something about...Kingman."

"Just my luck," Clay said and downed the rest of his beer.

Clay couldn't figure out why the man had confronted him the way he had. It was rather unusual that a man would take that approach with a total stranger. He couldn't help but wonder if there was more to it than he'd first thought. He soon found out.

Clay had one more beer before continuing his search for Bateman. He had traveled about a mile when he rounded a bend in the trail and caught some movement to his right above the trail.

He thought it might be a deer or some other wild animal, but then saw what had caught his eye. It was a horse...and it was saddled. As he continued to stare up the mountainside he noticed two other horses tied near the first one he'd seen.

He reined his horse to a halt sensing he might be riding into an ambush when a shot rang out. The bullet passed dangerously close to Clay's head causing him to dive off his horse and take cover behind a nearby rock.

He immediately drew his pistol and began scouring the mountainside hoping to spot his assailants. It didn't take long. A volley of gunfire was soon coming and echoed down the canyon trail. Butler held his position, but began looking for an escape route should he need to make a break for it.

Fortunately Butler's horse had not bolted when he dived from its back because his rifle was in his saddle scabbard. Based on the distance of the horses from the trail he'd need a rifle if he was to hit any of the bushwhackers.

"If you'll turn around and ride out of here, Butler, and promise to go back to Tucson, I'm sure the boys here will let you go," the third man called out.

"I thought that might be you, Bateman. As for going back to Tucson, when I go you'll go with me. It will be either in your saddle or across it, but you'll go back," Butler replied taking a hard line.

"Look, Crystal has been hurt before, but she always lands on her feet. Why, I'll bet you she's already got another partner lined up who has money to invest in her saloon," Bateman called back.

"We'll find that out when we get back down there, now won't we," Clay yelled back.

"Okay, but don't say I didn't give you a way out of this mess you're in now," Bateman answered.

Clay had to reach his horse and get his hands on his Winchester if he was going to have a chance in getting out of this mess. He quickly looked around for something he could use in getting his horse closer to him.

With the horse being only about ten feet away it wouldn't take much to give him a better chance of escaping this shootout. First, however, he would have to get his hands on his rifle.

"Come here, boy," Clay called in a loud whisper to his horse. "Come here."

This was the first time he had wished he'd taken the time to give his horse a name. He'd never been into that kind of thing all that much, because he went through a lot of horses in his line of work. He tried again.

"Come here, boy...want some sugar," he said remembering he'd picked up a several cubes at the last café he was in. He quickly felt in his shirt pocket and realized quickly that he only had one cube left due to giving them to his horse at each stop they'd made along the way.

The horse raised his head and looked in Butler's direction. Clay held out the sugar cube towards the horse and repeated, "Come on boy, come and get this sugar."

The horse moved closer to where Clay was hiding, but stopped several feet short of him. Just then Bateman called out again, "So what's it gonna be, Butler? Leave or die?"

"I'm going to leave, Bateman, but when I do, you're going with me," Clay answered back.

"You're a fool, Butler. I don't want to kill you, but you leave me no other choice," Bateman yelled back and then said to his two accomplices, "Let's go, boys."

Bateman and his two cohorts began moving cautiously down the mountainside in Butler's direction. Butler peered over the rock he was using for cover and noticed that the three of them would have to pass through a small stand of pines. When they did they would lose sight of him for a few seconds. It was then he would have to make his move.

When they came to the tree line Bateman remained in a spot where he could keep an eye on Butler's location. The other two men disappeared into the trees. Butler knew he had to make his move towards his horse right then.

Clay sprang out from behind the rock and made a mad dash towards his horse. Bateman hadn't expected the move but fired a quick shot that kicked up dust near Clay. Butler reached the horse and grabbed his Winchester out of the saddle scabbard. Turning quickly he made another dive back down to the rock for cover.

Bateman began firing rapidly, chips of the rock flying off as the bullets pinged off it. It was one of those chips that hit Butler in the eyes, blinding him for a moment. He instantly began rubbing his eyes which were tearing so much he couldn't see a thing.

Clay knew that he didn't have long before the two men in the trees would be in a position to begin firing at him. He blinked his eyes rapidly, hoping to clear them somewhat before it was too late. Butler muttered the words, "God help me."

His vision was blurred, but as he looked up the hillside again he could make out images just coming out of the wooded area. His vision was far from clear, but he could see somewhat.

Butler began firing his Winchester rapidly in the direction of the blurry images. It was the third shot fired that he heard a cry of pain. He had managed to hit one of the men. He didn't know which one and right then didn't care. He was merely glad that he had winged one of the ambushers.

Ever so slowly his vision began to clear and he actually could identify Bateman as he emerged from the tree line. Clay fired two quick shots and Bateman went down and didn't move.

The third man had managed to get to cover and called out to Clay, "Hey, I've got no quarrel with you. You just killed the man who hired us. My partner is gut shot and I've got to try and get him some help. Don't shoot. I'm going back up the hill for my partner."

"Go ahead, but one false move and it will be your last," Clay yelled back.

"Don't shoot...I'm coming out."

The man moved out from behind the log he had been hiding behind and headed back up the steep slope. Clay was still having trouble seeing clearly, but could tell the man was moving away. He waited until he saw the man pick up his partner before he moved out from behind the rock.

Clay moved up to where his horse was still standing and removed the canteen from the saddle horn. He quickly doused his eyes with water and washed the small rock fragments out. He could see much better then.

The two men made it back to their horses and rode away. Clay moved to a point where he could watch them and once he was sure they weren't doubling back on him moved up the hillside to where Bateman was laying.

Bateman was dead all right; a bullet through his heart. Clay looked up the hill a little higher and saw Bateman's horse tied to a small sapling. He went up to the horse and checked the saddlebags. The bags contained at least most of the money that Bateman had stolen.

After burying the man he'd shot, Butler mounted up and rode Bateman's horse down the mountain to where his horse was still feeding on some grass next to the trail. It was time for him to head back to Tucson.

Chapter 15

Sugarloaf Area
Tulare County, CA

Brent Sackett and the others in the Heller gang rode down a narrow trail headed north through an area called 'Sugarloaf'. Garth Heller wanted to stay in the mountains to avoid running into lawmen that might recognize the gang.

Heller's plan was to ride along the foothill range of the Sierra Nevada Mountain Range and when they reached an area called Squaw Valley they would head due west into Fresno.

Brent didn't like riding with a gang of wanted men and had to figure a way out of this situation. He suddenly had a brain storm and called out to Garth.

"Hold up, Garth. I have to tighten the cinch on my saddle," he said.

"Hold up, men," Garth said holding up his right hand.

Brent dismounted and began to fumble with the latigo on his saddle. When he had finished he looked at Garth and asked, "Do you have a map of this area?"

"Yeah, I have a map. Why?" Garth replied.

"I'd like to take a look at it if I may. I need to get a feel for this land around here," he stated.

"Okay," Garth said and reached inside his saddlebag and pulled a battered map out and tossed it to Brent.

After looking at the weathered map, Brent made a suggestion that he hoped Garth would go for.

"Look, Garth, if the gang keeps traveling together like we're doing, we're going to stand out like sore thumbs on a 'saw bones'. I see this town on the valley floor called Porterville. If half the gang cuts down to Porterville and then along the valley floor to Fresno, while the other half of the gang takes the higher route to this area called Squaw Valley we won't arouse suspicions nearly as much as all of us riding together."

"And I guarantee you that with all of us riding together; especially as well known as your gang is; someone will report it to a sheriff or a marshal before we ever get to Fresno," Brent said tightly.

Garth took on a serious expression as he mulled over Brent's suggestion. After careful consideration he called to the others.

"Listen up. We've got a change in plan. Here's what we're going to do," Garth said and proceeded to explain the plan to the others as though it was his own.

"Dooley, I want you Ned and Waco to go with Ben here into Porterville. Max, you and Jasper will go with me on up to Squaw Valley and come into

Fresno that way. Are there any questions?" Garth asked.

"Yeah, I've got one," Dooley said. "Why ain't I riding with you and Max? We've always rode together before," Dooley wanted to know.

"Because you know the way around the Porterville and Visalia area, Dooley, that's why. Ben isn't all that familiar with it and neither are Ned and Waco. We don't want to travel like we're a gang, we'd be spotted by the locals and they'd report it to the law," Garth snapped.

"Oh, okay Garth," Dooley said," I was just wondering, that's all."

Brent had to fight the urge to smile as Garth explained why they were splitting up. He'd have a much better chance of getting away from the gang if he was traveling with only half of them.

Garth turned to Brent and said, "There's a small settlement about fourteen or fifteen miles out of Porterville where we will split up. I'll take half the boys with me on up to Squaw Valley and you go with the others to Porterville. From there you can head north to Visalia and on up to Fresno. We'll meet up in Fresno at the Sierra View Saloon. It's a favorite of a lot of people so you won't have any trouble finding it."

"That sounds good to me. Once we meet up I'll get the fake bank inspection routine underway. This is going to be a piece of cake," Brent smiled.

Garth gave Brent a hard stare and said, "When you boys get to Visalia, be careful. It's a pretty rough town, if you get my drift. Keep an eye on the boys and don't let them take up with any women.

Once they get tanked up and have a woman on their arm they're hard to control."

"Don't worry about it. I'll keep a tight rein on them. The last thing we need right now is for someone to mess up. I need money and I'm sure you do too," Brent said firmly.

Garth grinned slightly and stated, "Ya know, Dalton...I wasn't too sure about you when we first met, but the better I get to know you, the more you seem all right to me."

"It could have been because of the badge I was wearing when we first met," Brent replied with a grin.

"Well, that may have been a major part of it," Garth said and laughed. He looked towards the other men and said under his breath, "When this job is finished I have an idea that calls for two men at the most. I think you're the man I need for that job. I don't want the others to know about it, so keep that under your hat."

"Can't you give me a hint as to what it's about?" Brent asked.

"Let's just say it's big, but two men can pull it off," Garth said with a wry grin.

"Okay, I'm interested."

The Sackett Ranch
Abilene, Texas

Brian and AJ stood by the corral watching Buster Leman busting a bronc. He was riding the pinto buck jumper and the other cowhands were hooting and hollering with each jump. Buster was a fairly new hire and it looked like the Sackett's had found a good hand.

Brian stood there silently watching the cowboy for over a minute. They could tell the horse was beginning to tire; the jumps were not nearly as violent as they had been. When the horse stopped bucking altogether, AJ shook his head and stated, "I don't know if that old saying is true, Brian."

"What old saying is that?"

"The one about there 'ain't a hoss ain't never been rode and there ain't a cowboy ain't never been throwed'. Buster there may be the exception to the rule," AJ said with a grin.

"He's got two good hands, he should be able to hang on," Brian said seriously.

AJ gave his brother a hard look and said tightly, "You're going to have to get over not being able to have full use of your right hand, Brian. These things happen and you know it. Look at Slim over there. He's got a bum leg, but he doesn't let it stop him from being a good cowhand.

"Junior there...he's only got one eye, but he's one of the best shots around. Plus he can spot things that a lot of people with three eyes would miss. They didn't just roll over and play dead and you're not going to either. Buck up, Brian," AJ said with a frown.

Brian looked at his brother and nodded, "Yeah, I know you're right, but I just never realized how much I do...or did...with my right hand. I can't even pen a letter anymore; not so it's easy to read anyway."

"How many letters do you write a year? You can still sign your name and that's about all you ever need to do working the ranch here," AJ said truthfully, but with a grin.

"I guess it's the handling of a gun. I thought I'd adjust to shooting left handed, but I don't see much improvement," Brian said looking at his left hand.

"Come on, I want you to talk to someone," AJ said and started around to the far side of the corral.

"Where're we going?" Brian asked.

"We're going to talk to Lefty Doyle. If anyone can tell you how to shoot left handed, it would be Lefty," AJ said as Brian walked up alongside him.

Lefty Doyle was an excellent shot with both a pistol and a rifle. He was very quiet about his past life before signing on with the Sackett brand, which led some to believe he may have been a man on the dodge. He had ridden for the brand for over two years.

Lefty did have a violent past, but he had always been on the right side of the law. In fact, he had worn a badge several times and built a reputation in parts of Kansas and Missouri. He had been a man much like Wyatt Earp. He pistol whipped more men than he shot; thanks to being close to them and much quicker on the draw than them.

AJ called to Doyle before they ever got to where he was standing with three other ranch hands. "Hey, Lefty...I've got a special job for you," AJ said.

"Oh, what's that, boss?" Lefty asked.

"I want you to teach Brian how to shoot left handed. Are you up to it?" AJ said with a chuckle.

"I don't think that will be hard at all. It's just like shooting with the right hand. It shouldn't take you long to make the switch Brian. I've seen you shoot. You probably didn't know that I'm actually right handed except when it comes to shootin'," Lefty said and grinned, exposing a missing tooth.

"No, I didn't know that," Brian said.

AJ grinned, "I knew it, where've you been little brother?"

"When do you want me to start with the pointers?" Lefty asked.

"There's no time like the present. Go out in back of the bunkhouse and do your practicing there. The horses are skittish enough as it is; what with this pinto buck jumper Buster just broke," AJ said.

Lefty and Brian headed for the backside of the bunkhouse and AJ glanced towards the ranch house. Two men had just ridden up to the front of the house. AJ recognized one of the men as the sheriff of Abilene.

"Now what could they want?" AJ said under his breath.

The sheriff and the man with him started for the front door when the sheriff saw AJ approaching from the corral and stop to wait for him. When AJ reached them the sheriff said with a serious look and said, "Hello AJ; is Brian around?"

"Yeah, he is. Why do you ask?" AJ questioned.

"Mr. Grover here just received a telegram from the front office of the railroad that Brian worked for and they want him to go back up to Wichita for a trial that's taking place up there. The telegram said Brian is one of the star witnesses in a plot to smuggle a cache of guns that were meant for some renegade Indians," the sheriff stated.

Mr. Grover then took over the conversation and explained the details.

"Brian and the gentleman who was training him met a woman who was supposedly taking her dead husband who'd died of cholera back to Texas by train. Well it turns out the woman and her husband had been running guns to the Indians for sometime. When the coffin her husband was supposed to be in fell off the loading platform and the cover came off they found the casket loaded with rifles."

"I see," AJ replied and paused for a moment in thought before asking the sheriff a question. "Well, that tells me why you're here Mr. Grover, but why did you have to come with him, Sheriff?"

"It's about your cattle. I got a report back that it isn't hoof and mouth disease they have; for lack of a better name, they're just calling it a cattle fever. I there's not a lot known about it, but it appears that some of your cattle are infected with it. Now I've got some good news," the sheriff said.

"Good news, eh," AJ said and then stated, "You tell us our cattle are infected with some fever and now you have good news for us? What is the good news that they're having a sale on cartridges in town?"

"No," the sheriff grinned and then chuckled, "nothing like that. The report I received and I'll give it to your pa, is that it's just the longhorns that have it. I know you have some, but fortunately for you it doesn't make up the bulk of your herd."

"No it doesn't. In fact, we only have about a hundred head of longhorns," AJ replied.

"Is your pa in the house?" the sheriff asked.

"Yeah, go on up. He'll be relieved to hear the report. I'll show Mr. Grover here where Brian is," AJ answered.

Just then two rapid shots rang out from behind the bunkhouse causing the three men to look in that direction. AJ grinned and said, "That sounds like Brian there," and laughed.

Raymond D. Mason

Chapter 16

December 8, 1879
Porterville, California

Brent and the other members of the Heller gang rode into the town of Porterville around five o'clock in the evening. They went directly to a saloon called Royal Porter's Bar and Dancehall. Brent told the others to go on inside and he'd join them later.

"Where are you going, Dalton? You don't know anyone around here," Dooley asked.

"I have to send a telegram to Fresno. I want to set the stage for the one we'll send just before we go in to take the bank. Does that meet with your approval, Heller?" Brent said tightly.

"Oh, I was just wondering, that's all. How long will you be?" Dooley asked.

"Not long, not long at all. I just have to find the telegraph office. It shouldn't be more than ten to twenty minutes at the most," Brent replied.

Brent waited until the men went inside and then reined his horse in the direction of the town's center. He planned to report the gang's intention to rob a bank. He'd turn this whole thing over to the local law and let them deal with it.

What Brent didn't know was that Dooley had entered the bar, but stood by the door and watched Brent ride off. He hurriedly mounted his horse and followed Brent at a safe distance. He watched as Brent entered the sheriff's office.

Brent showed the sheriff the deputy's badge he still had in his possession and told the sheriff he was working undercover to capture the Heller Gang. The sheriff was satisfied with Brent's story and took down all the information that Brent gave him.

Brent told the sheriff that he would continue to ride on to Fresno with the gang so they wouldn't get suspicious. Once they reached Fresno he would lead them to the bank and the law could take over from there. He also told him they were to meet up at the Sierra View Saloon.

Brent was relieved that the sheriff hadn't recognized him from the wanted posters that were being circulated. Perhaps he hadn't even received one yet. Whatever the reason Brent was thankful.

After giving the sheriff all the information about the gang and their plans, Brent mounted up and headed back to the bar where he'd left the others. He was totally unaware of the fact that he was being watched very closely by Dooley Heller.

When Brent left the sheriff's office Dooley crossed the street and peered through the sheriff's office window. He saw the sheriff seated at his desk and going over the information he'd written down from Brent's briefing. Dooley quickly looked up and down the street to make sure there was no one around before drawing his pistol and entering the office.

Upon hearing the door open the sheriff thought maybe it was Brent returning and before turning around said, "I was just going over the information you..." When he realized it wasn't Brent it was too late. Dooley shot the sheriff twice, killing him. He quickly rushed up to the desk and grabbed the paper the sheriff had been looking at and shoved it into his shirt.

Not wanting to be caught coming out of the sheriff's office, Dooley went out the side door into an alleyway. He ran to the narrow road behind the sheriff's corral and then to the next crossroad.

By the time Dooley got to where he could see the front of the sheriff's office a number of people were gathered at the office door and peering inside. Dooley casually walked up to the group and asked one of the men, "What happened?"

"Someone shot the sheriff," the man said never really looking at Dooley.

"Now who would do a terrible thing like that?" Dooley said and slowly walked across the street to where he'd tied his horse.

Rather than go back to Royal Porter's Bar, Dooley went to another small bar where he could read what the sheriff had written down. As he read a deep frown spread across his face. Once he'd finished reading the paper he folded it up and stuck it in his shirt pocket.

"Well, Ben Dalton or whatever your name is, you're in for a little surprise when we get to Fresno.

I'm sure Garth will have something special in mind for you," Dooley said under his breath.

When Dooley returned to Royal Porter's place Brent was seated with the other two gang members. Brent saw Dooley walk through the front door and motioned to him to let him know where they were sitting. Dooley pretended everything was okay and when Brent asked him where he'd been gave an answer that no one would doubt.

"I know this little gal that lives here in town and I went to see if she was home. She wasn't, that's why I'm back so soon," Dooley said getting a grin from Ned and Waco.

"I hope you won't make a habit out of drifting off like that, Dooley," Brent stated. "We don't want anyone getting into trouble and drawing a lot of undue attention to ourselves."

"You rode off...you know, to the telegraph office. Did you send the telegram?" Dooley asked.

"Yes, I did. Everything is going along just as planned," Brent said getting a wry grin from Dooley.

"That's good to hear," Dooley said forcing a smile.

"How far is it on over to Visalia?" Brent asked.

"Not far, around twenty five, twenty six miles I'd say," Dooley said and then asked, "Why, do you want to go on up there tonight?"

"No, we can head out tomorrow for Fresno. Garth was a little worried about us going to Visalia. We can make Fresno in a day's ride from here, can't we?" Brent asked.

"Yeah, we can. It's flat all the way," Dooley said just as someone burst through the front door and yelled out.

Brent couldn't make out what the man said at first, but when the man repeated himself he heard, "Someone shot Sheriff Crowder. He's dead," the man stated.

Brent's heartbeat quickened at the news. His first thought was about Dooley and his disappearance? Where had he really gone? He cast a quick look Dooley's way and caught the slightest of grins. When Dooley saw Brent looking his way he took on a look of surprise.

"Well look at that. Someone shot the sheriff of this one horse town. He must have had some enemies around," Dooley said looking at Ned and Waco.

Brent had an uneasy feeling about the sheriff being killed. He sensed that it was because of the information he'd left with him, especially with Dooley's late arrival back here at the saloon.

Brent had to set the stage for an excuse for being in the sheriff's office just in case Dooley had followed him there. Quickly he did just that.

"I just talked to that sheriff, too," Brent said.

His statement got the attention of the others, including Dooley.

"How'd it happen that you talked to the sheriff?" Waco asked.

"I was on my way to the telegraph office, but when I got there it was closed. I know that most sheriffs can have someone come down and open up, so that's why I went to speak with him.

"When I went in he recognized me from seeing me in Bakersfield. He wanted to know what I was doing up here and I told him I was undercover for the Kern County Sheriff.

"When I saw the wanted posters on his wall I realized just how recognizable the Heller boys are. He had all three of your posters on his wall, Dooley. I commented about it and he said they had word that the Heller gang was headed for Fresno to rob a bank there. He said he had it on good authority.

"That's when I decided to give him our plan and tell him I was working undercover. I told him I was traveling with several members of the gang and what we were planning. I didn't want us walking into a trap in Fresno. Garth didn't do a very good job of checking out that bank. Even the plan I laid out for him wouldn't work with what's waitin' up there," Brent said quickly.

Dooley hadn't expected a full confession from Brent and was somewhat confused as to what to do next. He looked from one man to the other trying to get his thoughts together. Brent then put him on the defensive.

"Dooley, have you or Max been shootin' your mouth's off about pulling a bank job up in Fresno? I'm sure Ned and Waco haven't been spoutin' off about it...have you boys?"

"No, we ain't told any one what our plans were, mainly because we didn't know about it until a few days ago," Ned said and looked at Dooley.

"Well, I have something to show you boys," Dooley said and pulled out the information the sheriff had written down.

"Look at this," Dooley said and laid the paper on the table.

Brent grinned slightly and then frowned as he shook his head slowly and said, "My, my I don't know how you Heller boys have avoided a noose for as long as you have. You killed the sheriff over this?"

"You gave him our whole plan," Dooley snapped.

"I just told you that, Dooley. That bank in Fresno has guards in and around it day and night until the large shipment has been distributed to other banks in the county. If we'd went in there with any plan we'd have been gunned down or arrested and hanged before we knew what hit us.

"So now you've got the law on us before we ever get word to Garth about what's happened. I don't think he's going to be too happy with you. I swear you boys are the dumbest 'badmen' I've ever had the misfortune of joining up with.

"I don't know about you, Ned and you Waco, but I'm clearing out of here before the law comes down on us with all four feet. Dooley, you fouled this up, so you go up and warn your two brothers about calling off the bank job," Brent said as though thoroughly disgusted with Dooley.

"I'm with you, Dalton. Waco, let's you and me head over to Monterey. I know some people over there that might have something going for us," Ned said getting an agreeing nod from Waco.

"As for me, I'm bypassing Fresno all together myself, Dooley. If you know what's good for you, you'll burn leather up to where your brothers are unless you want to see 'em both dead," Brent said seriously.

Dooley looked from one man to the other and then at the paper on the tabletop. He thought for a moment and then grabbed the paper off the table and shoved it in his pocket. Brent pretended to not care in the least.

"I'm taking this with me to show Garth," Dooley said.

"Go ahead, but don't forget to tell him what I told you. I think he'll see the worth in what I did. He's got a pretty good head on his shoulders," Brent said and added. "As for me, I'm leaving here tonight because the town's people are surely going to be asking strangers in town a lot of questions," Brent said as he stood up.

"We're with you, Dalton," Ned and Waco said and they too got up to leave.

"Adios, Dooley," Brent said and walked out of the saloon with Ned and Waco following after him.

Chapter 17

Brent told Ned and Waco goodbye as they mounted up to leave. Dooley walked to the saloon entrance with a dour look on his face and watched in silence as the three men headed out of town. Dooley hurriedly swung into the saddle and headed north. He was panic stricken as he thought about what Garth was going to say about all this.

Brent took a different road out of Porterville but headed north just the same. He didn't figure he'd have any trouble from the Heller gang anymore and all he wanted to do then was get on up to Sacramento.

The next stop on Brent's journey was the wild town of Visalia. He figured on getting a hotel room there and striking out early the next morning for the town of Stockton, but bypassing Fresno.

Dooley rode his horse hard until he came to a small cattle ranch about twenty miles north of Porterville. By the time he arrived there it was after midnight and his horse was winded.

Figuring on changing horses at the ranch, Dooley picked a buckskin stallion and had just saddled it and started on when the rancher suddenly ran out of his house and began shooting at him and yelling "Horse thief."

Several of the rancher's wranglers emerged from the bunkhouse and they too started firing. Several bullets struck Dooley and knocked him off the horse. He began firing at the rancher and his men but was soon hit again.

When the shooting stopped Dooley Heller lay dead on the ground. The paper he had killed the sheriff for had several bullet holes in it and was saturated with blood, making it impossible to read.

Brent took a room and slept until around 7 the next morning. He ate a hearty breakfast and headed north to Sacramento. When he came to Fresno he stayed to the west side and rode along with several wagons that were also heading north.

Brent couldn't get over how foggy it could get in the San Joaquin Valley. The fog, he learned, was called Tule fog. The fog would hug the ground but might only be eight to ten feet high; it could be very dense and cold.

It took him a couple of days but he finally made it to Sacramento. Not having any idea where Cheryl Keeling and the others might be, he figured the best place to start would be with some of the businesses they might have stopped in for supplies. He was unlucky with getting any information about them, even after he checked with a couple of banks and the newspaper office.

While in the newspaper office he had an idea of how they might find him. Brent ran an ad in the paper that simply read, 'Looking for Cheryl

Keeling. Leave word as to your whereabouts at the Sacramento newspaper office.'

He explained his situation to the editor of the newspaper who readily agreed to take any messages that might be left for Brent. Brent told the editor that he would be staying in the Sacramento Hotel should Mrs. Keeling answer the ad.

Brent paid for the ad to run for a month and then left the newspaper office and found a saloon and a poker game. It had been sometime since he'd felt free enough to sit down and really relax in a friendly game of poker. One of the men in the poker game, however, was a poor loser, as Brent would soon find out.

Creel Browner was a big man. He owned a slaughterhouse there in Sacramento and was known around town for his bad temper. Browner was slightly larger than Brent who stood 6'4" tall and weighed around 230 lbs.

Browner was not a good poker player. He took far too many chances and his bets were on the wild side. Brent had Browner figured very quickly and noticed something early on about Creel's mannerism when he had a good hand. Browner would tug at his ear.

As the game wore on so did Browner's temperament. He began to snap at the men in the game as his stack of chips began to dwindle away. Brent was the big winner at the table which didn't set well with Browner. Finally Creel had seen and had enough.

"I'm wondering about your dealing," Creel said looking across the table at Brent.

"Oh, and what is it you're wondering about it?" Brent said as he shuffled the cards.

"You sure catch a lot of good hands; but, they seem to come when you've got the deal," Browner said.

"Now, Creel that ain't right. He's just been lucky, that's all. He's won when any one of us was dealing," a man named Oral said.

"That makes me even more suspicious. I'm wondering if he might be palming cards, he seems the type," Creel said.

"Be very careful where you're taking this conversation and your accusations, big man. No one has to cheat to beat you. You're a lousy poker player as anyone at this table can see. I've watched you make bets a ten year old girl wouldn't make and now you're gettin' upset because you're losing," Brent said with a frown.

"I've played poker since I could hold a handful of cards, so don't tell me I don't know the game," Creel said, his face reddening slightly.

"I didn't say that you didn't know the game. I said you're a lousy poker player," Brent said evenly.

"Let's say I am a lousy player, I'll tell you what I am good at though," Browner growled.

"And what's that?" Brent asked.

"Breaking people's back," Creel said and started to stand up.

Brent slowly raised his Colt .44 up from under the table and said, "You ain't going to break my back. Not with a hole through your spine," Brent said giving Browner a hard glare.

Browner's eyes widened at first and then narrowed as he spat out the words, "I figured you for a gunny. Put that gun up and I'll show you how a real man handles himself."

"If I put this gun away you're going to get the beating of a lifetime. Now we can either finish playing cards, you can leave the game, or we can go outside and see if you can back up your mouth," Brent said.

Browner stood taller and said, "There's a place right outside the side door over there."

Brent looked towards the door and remembered noticing a narrow gap between the saloon and the building next to it. He figured Browner would have a definite advantage in close quarters, but Brent preferred to move around when he fought.

"I want the whole town to see you get your butt kicked, hoss. Let's take it right out into the street in front. I'm sure there are a lot of people around here that you've buffaloed and bullied enough to want to see you lose your pride along with a mouthful of teeth," Brent said with a slight grin.

Browner didn't say anything at first, but after thinking about Brent's words had second thoughts about the situation. Very few men had stood up to Browner before; most of them were much smaller than Brent which weighed heavily in Browner's decision.

"I'm not afraid of you, cheater, but I'd rather spend the time winning some of my money back," Browner finally said.

"You won't win it back. Not the way you bet and play your hands," Brent said evenly.

"We'll see about that," Browner said and slowly sat back down.

Brent didn't want to get into a skirmish with anyone here in Sacramento if he could avoid it. He was tired of running from the law and always looking over his shoulder. Hopefully Browner would cool down and the tension would wane.

The game continued and tempers did cool, but another form of tension began to build for Brent when the town marshal and three of his deputies entered the saloon and began moving slowly among the tables.

"Who are you looking for, Marshal?" someone called out to the marshal.

"Never mind Hershel, it ain't you," the marshal replied.

They moved closer to the table where Brent was seated causing him to keep his face turned away from them. When they reached his table the marshal said, "I'd like some identification, stranger."

Brent looked up prepared to give a response and realized the marshal had his back turned to him and was speaking to someone at the table next to the one where Brent sat. He breathed a sigh of relief.

Suddenly the man was addressing sprang to his feet and shoved one of the deputies into the marshal. He made a break for the door, but the other two deputies grabbed him as he ran past them. All three men fell over a table and onto the floor.

"Get the cuffs on him," the marshal yelled out.

The deputies got the man handcuffed and on his feet and started escorting him towards the front door, headed for jail. The marshal turned to Brent's table and touched the brim of his hat and said, "Sorry about that, boys. I hope we didn't ruin your game."

When they all said there was no harm the marshal started to turn and go, but did a double take and looked back at Brent. He cocked his head to one side and then to the other as he studied Brent carefully.

"Don't I know you from somewhere?" the marshal asked Brent.

"I've never been to 'somewhere'," Brent replied with a grin.

The marshal smiled slightly and said, "You're not from Utah are you?"

"Nope, Marshal…I've never been to Utah. I'm from Colorado," Brent replied, telling a half truth.

"Hmm, you sure look like a fella I knew in Utah. Oh, well, sorry I bothered you," the marshal said with another tip of the hat brim and followed his deputies out of the saloon.

Browner eyed Brent for a moment and the thought entered his mind that this stranger in town might very well be a man on the dodge. He'd have to do a little checking up on him, but first he'd have to learn the man's real name. The more he thought about it, the better the idea seemed to him.

Brent was relieved that no more was made out of the encounter than had just occurred. His main concern now was locating Cheryl Keeling and the others. He hoped she would see the ad in the newspaper and respond quickly. Until then all he could do was wait. And waiting was something he was not good at.

One of the men at the table chuckled and said, "Tom is always thinking he knows someone from Utah."

"What's the marshal's name?" Brent asked.

"Tom Farrell...from Utah," the man said getting a laugh from everyone at the table with the exception of Browner.

Chapter 18

The Sackett Ranch
Abilene, Texas

Brian rode into the Sackett barnyard dragging a small tree behind his horse. His father walked out onto the porch and smiled.

"There's something following you there, son," John said.

"Yeah, I know, Pa. I can't seem to shake it. It's followed me for over ten miles," Brian grinned.

"What is it, do you know?" John asked.

"I think they call it a Christmas tree," Brian said as he climbed down off his horse.

"Hmm, what do you do with them?" John asked feigning seriousness.

"I've heard you decorate 'em and stand them in your house to celebrate the birth of the Christ Child," Brian said, going along with the tease.

"Well, bring it on in and let's start decoratin' that thing," John laughed.

"Hey, I went and got it. You and the others can decorate it. I swear I have to do everything around this ranch," Brian said ribbing his dad.

John laughed as he went out to help Brian bring the tree inside the house. They lugged the tree indoors and laid it in the big living room. John suddenly remembered something and said quickly, "Oh, I almost forgot, Brian. Someone left a letter with your name on it at the general store. I guess they knew we'd be coming in this morning."

"Who'd write a letter to me and leave it at the general store, I wonder?" Brian asked aloud.

"Who do you know who can write, is more like it," AJ said as he entered the room and got in on the tail end of the conversation.

"The same people you know, AJ," Brian replied with a laugh.

Brian opened the letter and began to read. The moment he realized who the letter was from he sneaked a quick peek in AJ's direction. AJ was busy looking at the tree and wasn't paying any attention at all to Brian's reading of the letter.

Brian walked slowly out of the room while reading what was contained in the letter. He stopped when he reached the staircase and looked somberly down at the paper. He cast a quick glance back towards the living room and at AJ.

The letter was from Terrin Gibbons; the woman Brian had been in love with, but had parted company when he found out about another man in Terrin's life. Now AJ had begun seeing her and it appeared that Terrin wanted to talk to Brian...alone.

After reading the letter Brian slowly folded it up and stuck it in his shirt pocket. He certainly didn't want to hurt AJ by sneaking around and seeing Terrin. She had said in the letter that she wanted to speak with him and try to explain her side of what had caused their breakup. Brian wanted to hear what she had to say, but was concerned that AJ might find out about the rendezvous.

He decided to meet her at the place and time she had suggested in the letter. She said she would wait one hour for him and if he didn't show up she would assume he had no interest in seeing her again.

Brian knew the spot Terrin had suggested. The two of them had picnicked there on several occasions. Of course he'd with meet her. He knew in his heart that he hadn't completely gotten over her yet.

Sacramento, CA

Brent hadn't heard a word from Cheryl Keeling. He had checked back with the newspaper office several times, but no word yet. He spent most of his day playing poker in the Gold Nugget Saloon.

One evening a new face walked up to the table and asked if there was an open seat in the game. The man was told there was and when he sat down Brent noticed a badge pinned to the man's shirt, but hidden from view under his coat.

Brent had never seen the man before so he didn't feel he was in any danger. Once the marshal began talking, however, Brent grew slightly more nervous. The marshal introduced himself as Earl Haddock.

"So what brings you to Sacramento, Marshal?" one of the men in the game asked.

"Several things, actually," the marshal said with a slight grin. "I had some business to take care of here in town. I'll be heading back down to the Los Angeles area tomorrow."

As the game got underway the marshal picked up on Brent's Texas drawl and then noticed how much Brent fit the description of the man described on wanted posters as being Brent Sackett. The marshal knew Sackett was supposed to have died during a jailbreak, but the man's face had been blown away and could have been just about anyone.

Finally the marshal looked at Brent and asked, "You look familiar, partner; what's your name?"

Brent forced a smile as he replied, "Ben Tanner, Marshal."

The marshal pondered the name for a moment and then said, "Nope, I must have you mixed up with somebody else. Let's play some poker, what do ya' say?"

Brent went on another winning streak and soon forced the marshal out of the game. The other players had a slightly larger bankroll than the marshal and stuck around. Before the night was over Brent walked away with over five hundred dollars.

The sun was just topping the Sierra Nevada Mountain Range when Brent walked out of the saloon and headed for his hotel room. As he walked along he pondered the fact that he was taking on too many aliases and they could come back to haunt him.

He didn't know it at the time, but that is just what was about to happen. When Brent got back to his hotel room he started across the hotel lobby when someone called out his name; his real name.

"Brent? Brent Sackett...is that you?" the man said as he walked out of the hotel restaurant.

Brent snapped his head around quickly at the calling of his name and found himself staring into the face of a man he'd served with in the Confederate army. The man's name was Captain Harley Jennings; Brent's commanding officer.

Brent looked around quickly to see if anyone was within earshot of the two and one he determined no one could hear them greeted the captain.

"Captain Jennings! It is such an honor to see you again. How have you been and what brings you out to California?" Brent asked as the two shook hands.

"It's good to see you, also. I would imagine the same thing lured me out West that brought you out here. A chance to cash in on the fortune to be made out here," the captain replied.

"I take it you moved your family out here from Tennessee?" Brent queried.

"No, not yet," the captain said before adding, "I will be sending for them as soon as I get a place for us to live. So tell me, what are you up to these days?"

"Actually, Captain, I'm trying to locate some people I helped move out here. We got separated after we reached California and we're supposed to meet up here in Sacramento," Brent explained.

"Do you mean to tell me you aren't married yet? I never thought of you as a ladies man. I thought you would be the type to find a good woman and settle down," the captain grinned.

Brent took on a slightly more serious look as he replied, "I was married, but my wife was killed on the way out here."

The captain's eyes widened, "Oh, Brent...I'm so sorry. I didn't mean to sound so flippant."

"Hey, it's okay. You had no way of knowing, Captain. Actually she was shot while we were fleeing from a gang of outlaws in New Mexico. I look at my time with her, as short as it was, to have been the best time of my life," Brent said sincerely.

"That sounds like something you would say, Brent," the captain said and then asked. "Are you staying here at the hotel?"

"Yes, I am, as a matter of fact."

"I'll tell you what, let's have supper together. I just finished breakfast or I'd invite you to a meal. The food here is quite good, I must say."

"Supper sounds good to me," Brent said with a smile.

"Okay, let's say around six o'clock right here," the captain suggested.

"Six o'clock it is," Brent said and shook the captain's hand again.

Brent watched the captain walk away and remembered what a good commanding officer he'd been during the War. He'd always pondered any decisions he had to make and didn't plunge his men into something they had no chance of surviving.

Brent went up to his room and washed up before going to bed. He slept for around six hours, got up, dressed and went back to the newspaper office. There was still no response from Cheryl on his ad, so he decided to look around Sacramento and see what this town was really like.

At precisely six o'clock that evening the captain met Brent at the entrance to the hotel restaurant. They were seated at a table in the middle of the large room which made Brent a little bit nervous. He liked sitting with a wall at his back. The captain noticed how Brent kept looking around their surroundings.

The captain chuckled, "Old habits die hard don't they Brent."

"They sure do. What about you? Do you still have issues you brought home from the War?"

"Oh, yeah, plenty of them," the captain said seriously. "My wife says I talk in my sleep, calling out the names of some of the men under my command. She says I'm calling out loudly and telling them to 'watch out' or 'get down'."

"That was like going through hell. It changed a lot of men, I can tell you that," Brent said.

The waiter came and gave them a menu and said he'd be back shortly. As the two men surveyed the choices two men entered the restaurant. It was the Tom Farrell, the local marshal and Marshal Earl Haddock.

As the maitre de escorted the two lawmen to their table they passed by the table occupied by Brent and Captain Jennings. Brent saw the two men and dropped his napkin in an effort for them to pass by without recognizing him. It almost worked.

Marshal Haddock glanced at the man bending over in an effort to retrieve his napkin and stopped long enough to bend down and pick it up. As he handed it to Brent he broke into a wide grin.

"Well, hello again Tanner. Are you going to be playing cards again later on? I'd like to get into your pocket this time," the marshal said with a grin.

Marshal Farrell stopped and eyed Brent as well. He smiled as he said, "Oh, yeah...the man I thought I knew from Utah. How's it going?"

"Fine, fine...uh, yeah, Marshal I'll be playing cards again later on and at the same saloon," Brent said casting a quick glance in Captain Jennings direction.

"I'll see you there, Tanner," Marshal Haddock said and the two moved on to their table.

The captain didn't say anything about the name, but Brent knew he'd caught it. He looked down and then looked directly into the captain's face.

"I guess you noticed that, huh?"

"Yeah, I did. Do you want to talk about it?"

Brent took a deep breath before saying, "I got into a little trouble back in Texas and that's part of the reason I'm out here. I've had to take on a couple of new names to try and throw the law off my trail. I'm not proud of what I did, but I can't change it now."

The captain nodded slowly and said, "We're all running from ghosts in our past, Brent. Your secret is safe with me. If there's anything I can do to help you, just let me know."

"I will, Captain…and thank you for that," Brent replied.

"Let's not let the past mar the present, what do you say?"

"I'm all for that, Captain. In fact, tonight's supper is on me," Brent smiled and then added. "Let me rephrase that…tonight's supper is on the marshal who just stopped by here."

Brent's remark brought a grin from the captain and then they both broke into laughter. It was good to laugh. Brent felt a huge weight lift off his shoulders in knowing that the captain was willing to leave the past where right where it was; in the past.

The two of them enjoyed a great dinner and a bottle of fine wine. Afterwards they ordered coffee and the captain pulled out two long cigars for their enjoyment. They talked for over an hour before finally saying goodnight. The captain headed down the street to see a play at the Sacramento Theater and Brent headed for the poker game with Marshal Haddock.

Raymond D. Mason

Chapter 19

Brent had another good night at cards walking away with over two hundred and fifty dollars. He returned to his hotel and got to bed around midnight. He slept very soundly, but was up by six o'clock in the morning and went down to the restaurant for breakfast.

Just as he reached the top of the staircase to start down he noticed three adults and two children enter the lobby. One of the two women was carrying a small baby. His heart jumped when he realized it was Cheryl Keeling and the others who were just entering the hotel.

They didn't see Brent until he reached the bottom of the staircase, but when they did, Hank and Annie Thurston ran across the lobby to greet him. They hugged him around the waist as they looked up at him wide eyed. Cheryl, Grant Holt and Daysha Jones also hurried up to where Brent had stopped wearing wide smiles on their faces as well.

Everyone started talking at once causing Brent to laugh and say, "Hold on there...one at a time. Go ahead Cheryl, tell me what all happened. How was your trip up here?"

"After the episode with the outlaw gang it went very smoothly," Cheryl said, causing Brent to look at her questioningly.

"What's this about an outlaw gang?" Brent replied.

"I'll tell you all about it once we get to where we're staying," Cheryl said, all smiles, but then paused and asked. "You are going with us, aren't you?"

"Yes, I am. Well, at least to see where you are staying and make sure you get settled in somewhere permanently," Brent replied

"Oh...I see," Cheryl said, her disappointment showing in her pretty blue eyes.

"Hey, none of that now; besides, who knows how long that may take," Brent said with a warm smile.

Daysha who was holding Grant's baby moved closer to Brent and said, "Look how much the baby has grown since the last time you seen her."

Brent gazed at the baby and couldn't hold back a smile. He touched the baby's chin and she grinned up at him. Brent cast a quick glance towards Grant and said, "She's more beautiful than before, Grant." He then added, "It's good to see you again...all of you."

Brent glanced around the lobby at the onlookers and said quickly, "Come on, let's go in the restaurant where we won't be so conspicuous and where we can talk. I'll treat you to a fine breakfast, how's that?"

"You won't have to beg me," Grant said with a grin.

"Me neither," Daysha agreed.

"I'm starved," Hank said.

Cheryl laughed and said, "You had breakfast before we left the wagons."

"Yeah, but this is a real live restaurant," Hank said getting a laugh from the others.

"Can I have hot cakes?" Annie asked.

"You can have anything your little heart desires," Brent said.

They went into the restaurant where Cheryl filled Brent in on their adventure with the outlaw gang. Brent explained to them how he'd gotten away from the Texas Rangers by breaking out of the makeshift jail where they'd left him.

It was a wonderful reunion and Brent was so glad to see all of them. He was surprised at how much he'd missed them all; even Daysha who hadn't been with them all that long. Still, it was like a family getting back together.

Brent had the feeling that he was going to be here in California for a long, long time. If he could hide from his past he could actually begin a new life. He was especially glad to see Cheryl. Only now, after having been apart for awhile, did he realize how much she meant to him.

His feelings for her were not like they'd been for Julia, but there was definitely a connection between the two of them. He could tell she felt the same about him. Not by any words she'd uttered, but by the look in her eyes when she looked at him.

Yes, this could be the place where he would settle down and make a new life. He'd look around and find the best place to build a home. It felt good to see a future that wasn't painted black. No, his future out here in California would be painted 'gold', to match the 'Golden State'.

The End

Look for the next book in the Sackett series, to be titled:

"Sackett Bounty"

Books by This Author

8 Seconds to Glory
A Distant Thunder
A Tall Dark Stranger
Abilene Town
Along the Rio Hondo
An Invitation to Murder
A Motive for Murder
A New Man in Christ
A Tale of Tri-Cities
A Walk on the Wilder Side
Aces and Eights
Across the Rio Grande
American Knights: Immigrant
American Knights: Patriot
Between Heaven and Hell
Beyond Missing
Beyond the Great Divide
Beyond the Picket Wire
Blossoms in the Dust
Brimstone; End of the Trail
Brotherhood of the Cobra
Corrigan
Counterfeit Elvis (Welcome)
Counterfeit Elvis (Suspicious)
Counterfeit Elvis (Ghetto)
Dark Moon Rider
Day of the Rawhiders
Five Faces West
Four Corners Woman
Guns of Vengeance Valley
If Looks Could Kill
Illegal Crossing
Incident at Medicine Bow
In the Chill of the Night
King of the Barbary Coast
Laramie
Last of the Long Riders
Living by Faith, Hope, Love
Man from Silver City
Moon Stalker
Most Deadly Intentions
Murder on the Oregon Express
Night of the Blood Red Moon
Night Riders

Odor in the Court
On a Lonely Mountain Road
Purple Dawn
Quirt Adams (Dark Vengeance)
Range War
Rage at Del Rio
Rebel Pride
Return to Cutter's Creek
Ride the Hard Land
Ride the Hellfire Trail
Ride the High Sierra
Send in the Clones
Seven Guns to the Border
Shadows of Doubt
Showdown at Lone Pine
Since I Don't Have You
Sleazy Come, Sleazy Go
Streets of Durango: The Lynching
Streets of Durango: The Shootings
Suddenly, Murder
Summer Kisses, Winter Tears
Tales of Old Arizona
The Long Ride Back
The Murders on Music Row
The Mystery of Myrtle Creek
The Relentless Gun
The Return of 'Booger' Doyle
The Secret of Spirit Mountain
The Tootsie Pop Kid
The Woman in the Field
Three Days to Sundown
To Mock a Killing Bird
Too Late To Live
Yellow Sky, Black Hawk

Books in italics are *not* Westerns